100

D1394006

R

APACHE DAWN

Philip Ketchum was born in Trinidad, Colorado. A graduate from the University of Denver, he was employed for several years as a social worker. He started writing Western fiction for pulp magazines and by 1938 had become a regular contributor to Street and Smith's *Western Story Magazine*. Ketchum's first Western novel, *Texan on the Prod* (Popular Library, 1952), was an expansion of the story by the same title that had appeared in *Two Western-Action Books* (Summer, 1951). Later on in the decade his novels began being serialized in magazines, such as "Six-Gun Maverick" (Popular Library, 1957) in *Ranch Romances* in 1956. In the books Ketchum wrote beginning in the late 1950s, he moved away from easy plot resolutions and introduced a note of cynicism and grimness not found in his earlier stories. In *The Hard Man* (Avon, 1959), the searching protagonist finds that virtually the entire town had been somehow connected with his father's murder and his ultimate victory is not without a profound emotional cost. Ketchum's Western novels of the 1960s moved further in the direction of emotional realism. The settings are out of the ordinary, the characters drawn with depth, and plot developments grow out of internal necessity rather than the external constraints expected in traditional Westerns. Among his most exceptional novels are *Apache Dawn* (1960), *The Night Riders* (1966), *Gila Crossing* (1969), and *The Cougar Basin War* (1970). It is above all on stories such as these that Ketchum's recognition as a Western author of considerable stature can be said to rest.

APACHE DAWN

Philip Ketchum

GUNSMOKE

First published in the US by Avon Books

This hardback edition 2013
by AudioGO Ltd
by arrangement with
Golden West Literary Agency

Copyright © 1960 by Philip Ketchum.
Copyright © renewed 1988 by the Estate of Philip Ketchum.
All rights reserved.

ISBN 978 1 471 32142 9

British Library Cataloguing in Publication Data available.

Leabharlann
Chontae Uibh Fhaili

Class:
Acc:
Inv:

Printed and bound in Great Britain by
TJ International Limited

Chapter I

FROM THE EDGE of the trees crowning the hill, Jerd
Galway studied the narrow valley below. The circling buzzards which had attracted his attention were dropping
lower. Now, as he watched, two settled down on a crag of
rocks. Another sank below a screen of mesquite. Between them, lying in the clumpy grass, was an indistinguishable figure. It might be an animal—it could be a
man. From this distance he wasn't sure.

For several minutes then, he scanned the surrounding
area. In the past few days he hadn't seen anyone, or the
smoke of another fire. He had thought he was alone in
the hills, but he couldn't be certain. One of the posse
might have followed him. One of the prices of freedom,
so far as he was concerned, was constant vigilance, and
now he made sure he could see no other movements
anywhere. Assured of that finally, he put his horse down
the slope, angling toward the figure he had seen.

As he drew nearer, the buzzards took flight, beating the
air with their heavy wings and squeaking in protest. But
Jerd scarcely noticed them. His eyes were fixed on what
he had found—the motionless figure of a man. From his
garb, an Indian. Possibly one from the nearby reservation. A Chiricahua Apache.

Jerd reined up. He dismounted and walked toward the
figure. Almost at once he could tell the Indian was dead.
He had been shot through the body. But more than that,
he had been mutilated. Both ears had been sliced off.
Jerd stiffened. Of his own knowledge, he could think of
only one man who might have done such a thing. Clem
Driggs!

Instinctively, Jerd took another quick look up and
down the valley and at the bordering hills. An icy chill ran
down his back. If Clem Driggs was anywhere near, he was
in real danger. The man disliked him—and had for
years. Driggs could move silently as a shadow. He was

5

deadly with his rifle, and an expert with his knife. Driggs had once been a civilian scout with the army, but he had been discharged several months before and recently had been in Wickenburg. It wasn't at all unlikely that he might have joined the posse which had chased Jerd into the barrens. And very possibly, Driggs could have stuck to the trail, all the way up into the hills.

If he was nearby, however, he didn't show himself, and after a brief hesitation, Jerd stooped close to the Indian and rolled him over. He knew a number of Chiricahua Apaches but this one he didn't recognize. He had been an old man, thin, wrinkled. He had been shot in the back, and with no chance to defend himself—which wouldn't have worried Driggs. The scout hated the Indians. Any Indians. One of the reasons for his attitude toward Jerd had been that for years Jerd had lived with the Chiricahuas. So far as Driggs was concerned, such a stain could never be wiped out.

The buzzards still circled above. Jerd glanced that way, then, stooping again, he lifted the Indian's body, carried him to the nearby rocks, and lowered him to the ground. For the next few minutes he was busy, piling a rock cairn over the Indian's body. It struck him that if Driggs saw him doing such a thing, it would seem final proof that he was more Indian than white. But to hell with Driggs.

After the cairn was finished Jerd walked back to where he had found the Indian's body. He then spent several minutes reading the signs he could find. He did this partially by horseback and when he was through he could guess what had happened. The Indian had been riding down the valley when he was shot, and he had fallen to the ground. His unshod horse had strayed west. Driggs, if it had been Driggs who killed the Indian, had fired at him from a screen of shrubbery, up valley. Then, riding a shod horse, Driggs had approached the Indian's body and had dismounted to slice off the ears. He had worn moccasins, but that was natural to him.

Following the murder and the mutilation of the Indian, the man responsible had left the scene, riding down valley, southwest. At a guess, this had happened about four

hours earlier. That would have been at about nine
o'clock this morning.

Jerd took a look at his watch. It was an hour past
noon. Most of a long afternoon lay ahead. In these
rugged Mesquite hills, Driggs wouldn't travel very fast.
Particularly, he wouldn't travel fast if he was on a hunt.
Too easily, Jerd could catch up with him. Too easily, he
could get what the Indian got—a bullet in the back. In
the hours ahead, he was going to have to be damned careful.

He turned down valley, following Driggs' trail. Where
the hills closed in, the trail slanted south, climbing
through a sparse stand of stunted oak marked here and
there by yellow pines and a few juniper shrubs. Over
the crest of the rise he dropped down to a small stream.
The man he was following hadn't stopped there, but Jerd
did. It was time to do some thinking, some planning.

He dismounted, had a drink, refilled his canteen, then
rolled a cigarette—a tall man in buckskins and moccasins.
He had a thin, wiry frame, a narrow face, and rugged features. His nose was humped, his eyes were deep-welled
in his skull, his lips were full but straight, and his skin was
tanned—Indian tanned. Clem Driggs, of course, thought
him a breed. Driggs had never accepted the story that he
had been captured as a child by the Indians. But again
—to hell with Driggs.

Hunkering down in the shade near the stream, Jerd
took a brief look at the past. He had been reared as a
child with the Indians, had been turned back to his own
people under a treaty agreement, then as a young man he
had worked on a cattle ranch. Following that, he had
served the Army for a time, working as a civilian scout.
Next he had prospected, then drove a stage and, finally,
he had settled down on a homestead. Then one day, only
a few months ago, he had been arrested for a stage holdup, and had been tried and convicted. It was when the
sheriff tried to transport him to Yuma prison that he escaped. That had happened ten days ago.

Jerd finished his cigarette. He pinched out the fire,
dropped it, then shifted uneasily, scowling at the stream.
He thought he could understand why he had been arrested, but he hadn't been able to do anything about it.

What he could do now that he was free, he wasn't sure. Sam Rogell, who must have been the man responsible for his arrest, was a powerful figure in the Territory. To trap him wouldn't be easy. But, to be realistic, he had no time right now to think about Sam Rogell. It was much more important to think about Clem Driggs.

When Jerd came across the Indian, he had been sifting through the fringing Mesquite hills, heading east in the direction of the Sierra Robles. Driggs, from his present course, was traveling west, which might indicate he had lost the trail he had been following, and that he had been cutting back. But however he thought of it, Driggs was somewhere in the area, and on a manhunt. *Most of the time he'll stay between the hills,* Jerd decided. *Each mile or so, he'll climb to a high spot, and look around. He'll listen and watch, and most likely he noticed the buzzards; noticed that they started to settle down—but didn't. That will warn him that someone found and covered the Indian's body.*

If that was true, Jerd was going to have to watch every step he took. Quite possibly, if Driggs had noticed the buzzards, he would have turned back. Or, to look at it in another way, he and Driggs might be riding toward each other. Maybe they were a couple of hours apart. Maybe less.

Jerd checked his holster gun, his rifle, made sure his sheath-knife was in place, then mounted and rode on, following Driggs' trail. It led him over the shoulder of the next hill. Stretching ahead of him was a long, twisting valley between two hogbacks. Driggs seemed to have aimed at the open floor of the valley but Jerd reined up, scanned either side, then chose the north hogback as the one offering the best covering. He slanted that way. In half an hour he dropped down into the valley to make sure he hadn't lost the trail he was following. Assured that he hadn't, he climbed back under the screening trees.

This valley turned into another, but one that was wider, even more open, and neither flanking ridge was heavily wooded. That was because they had drifted to the fringing hills just above the barrens. Jerd pulled up again. He studied the terrain ahead. Considering what he knew of Clem Driggs and fearing the man might have turned back, Jerd didn't want to venture into the open country ahead. At too many places along the way, a man could be hiding, his rifle ready for use.

After a few minutes, Jerd drew back. He dismounted, tied his horse, then moved forward to a vantage point where he could stay hidden but still watch the valley. Settling down, he waited. An hour passed—part of another. The sun dropped lower. In the branches nearby, the tree birds, now used to his presence, made a constant chatter. The birds, the whispering wind and the crackling of dead wood were a normal cacophony of sound. Up the valley, nothing moved.

Another hour went by. The sun sank lower. The valley seemed deserted. But actually it hadn't been deserted. At a point hardly half a mile away, a man suddenly rode in sight, coming from a clump of trees which had hidden him. A slight, hunched figure in buckskins, and wearing an old grey campaign hat. *Clem Driggs!* From here, Jerd couldn't see his face, but he was sure he hadn't been wrong in his identification. It made him shaky to realize how close the man had been all afternoon. It made him shaky to realize what might have happened if he had started up the valley ahead. He would have had no warning about where the man was.

Jerd didn't move as Driggs rode into the open although his hand tightened on his rifle. And he wasn't surprised when Driggs pulled up at the next clump of trees. He could guess, almost exactly, what was in the man's mind. Looking back, Driggs had seen the buzzards fly away. From that, he had known someone had found the Indian. Curious as to who it was, he had turned back, part way, and had been watching his trail. A minute ago he had decided he had waited long enough, and that no one was following him. But he wasn't sure. He was still a little nervous, a little uncertain.

After a brief delay, Driggs rode on, almost directly toward Jerd. Steadily, the distance between them lessened. And now, as the man drew nearer, Jerd could see Driggs' leathery, wrinkled face, the bump of his nose, and the bony angle of his jaw. He was an ugly man—and ugly inside. When he had been a civilian scout, no one else would bunk with him. He smelled too much, from his own filth and from his box of trophies—human ears. He had been ordered to stop collecting them but it was well known that he hadn't.

When the man was only a dozen yards away, Jerd raised his rifle. His words were harsh. "That's far enough, Driggs. Shove your arms in the air."

Driggs didn't question the order. He reined up, jerked his arms in the air. In one hand he was clutching his rifle. And strangely, he didn't seem worried. "That you, Jerd? Knew you was somewhere around."

Jerd got to his feet. He stepped in sight, and kept his rifle on Driggs. "Don't know why I don't shoot you," he said flatly.

"That's easy. We been friends," Driggs said. And he started lowering his arms.

"I said, keep 'em up," Jerd whipped. "Damnit, do you want a bullet?"

Driggs' arms shot up in the air again, but he looked puzzled and he said, "Jerd, what's wrong? I'm plumb peaceful about you. Why do you think I'm here?"

"I'd like to know," Jerd said. "But first, drop your rifle, then your holster gun, then your knife. After that, swing to the ground."

"Seems damned unreasonable," Driggs said. But he did as he had been ordered—dropped his rifle, his holster gun, and his knife. Following that, he slid to the ground.

"Now lie down on your face," Jerd told him.

The man scowled, his lips working. "No sense in it. If you'd only listen a minute . . ."

"Down on your face. Now!"

Still grumbling, Driggs stretched out on the ground, and as he lay there, Jerd bound his wrists and ankles. Next, he tied the scout's horse and collected his weapons. When this had been done, Jerd had a cigarette, and wondered what to do with his prisoner. Normally he could have turned him over to the sheriff, charged with the murder of the Indian. But as things stood now, if he went anywhere near the sheriff he would be arrested himself.

"You ready to listen?" Driggs asked.

Jerd shrugged. "Go ahead."

"The general wants to see you."

"Like hell."

"Nope. That's the truth. The general wants you to arrange a palaver with Namacho."

Jerd sucked on his cigarette. It was quite possible that the general might have wanted to arrange a meeting with Namacho, and under ordinary circumstances, Jerd might have been asked to help. When he had lived with the Apaches, he had been reared in the same family as Namacho. In effect then, he and Namacho were brothers. They had gone through their puberty rites together. They had learned the same games, the same rules of hunting and fighting. They had been boyhood friends and, possibly, he could have set up a meeting between Namacho and the general. What good it would accomplish, however, was another matter. Namacho, after fleeing from the reservation, had led a raiding party down through the Dragoons and into Mexico. Then he had returned, and was now in the Sierra Robles, cooking up more trouble for the white people in the Territory. His course had been determined.

"You ain't been listening," Driggs complained. "I tell you, the general sent me."

"Nope, you're a bounty hunter," Jerd answered. "You came here, probably, because Sam Rogell put up a reward for my capture."

"Honest to God, you're wrong."

"You were kicked out as a scout. The general wouldn't have hired you again."

"But he did—just for this one job. To find you, Jerd. Do you know what Namacho's doin'? He's sent messengers to the Mimbres, to the Mescaleros, and several tribes. He's tryin' to stir up the entire Apache nation. If that happens . . ."

"You killed an Indian this morning. Why?"

Driggs shook his head. "Who cares about another Injun?"

"He was an old man, not a warrior."

"Still an Injun. Damnit, Jerd. Lemme go. I ain't done nothin' against you. When you see the general . . ."

"I'm not going to see the general."

"Then what about me?"

"I don't know about you," Jerd confessed. "Maybe I should . . ."

He broke off, raised his head, and stood listening. The birds in the trees above them had again hushed their singing as though they had been frightened away. Jerd looked from side to side. He could see nothing unusual but he knew instinctively something was wrong.

Driggs' voice was husky, whispered. "Jerd, cut me free. Gimme a gun. I tell you . . ."

An Indian stepped suddenly in sight from behind a screen of shrubbery. He was followed by another, and then another. And now from other, more distant points, more crouching figures appeared, and came forward. Possibly as many as twenty. Chiricahua Apaches—young braves, their faces painted with war markings. Some held spears or bow and arrow but fully a dozen carried rifles.

Jerd stood motionless. His rifle was in his hand, but he didn't raise it. To use it, he knew, would be fatal. These men, now circling them, had trapped them neatly. Perhaps, if Jerd hadn't been listening to Driggs, he might have heard the Indians creeping forward. Even so, however, he might not have escaped.

"We're dead men," Driggs said, and his voice was shaky. "If you hadn't tied me . . ."

Jerd scarcely noticed what Driggs had said. His eyes had settled on one of the Indians, a man now stepping in front of the others. He recognized him instantly. The man was Namacho.

Chapter II

HE WORE OLD, worn clothing, snagged and torn. A short man, stocky, wide-shouldered, thick-necked. His black hair was held down by a headband. He had thick features, his dark eyes heavily browed above a flat nose and wide lips. Staring at him, Jerd could read nothing in the Indian's expression. But that wasn't strange. Of his own knowledge he remembered that Namacho showed his feelings only in moments of exaltation, or in the bitterness of a defeat.

Half a dozen steps away, Namacho stopped. He spoke in his own tongue. "Hello, my brother. I did not think to find you in these hills."

"Am I not welcome, my brother?" Jerd answered, following the pattern Namacho had established. "Once we rode these hills together."

"That was long ago. Times have changed."

"For both of us."

"Yes, I have heard of your trouble," the Indian nodded. "One of our women who works among your people has told me of your arrest. It would have been better for you if you had stayed with us. There is still a place for you in my lodge."

Jerd was silent for a moment. He was surprised by the offer. He couldn't accept it, he knew, but neither could he reject it too quickly. To do so would be insulting. After a brief delay he spoke slowly. "This, my brother, is a thing which should be weighed carefully. It has been years since my ways have been yours."

"That is true," Namacho agreed. "I would not have asked you to return to my lodge if all had been well. But your own people have rejected you. I find you hiding in the hills, living as an animal. You will be pursued by your enemies. You will be caught and killed, I can offer you a finer death—the death of a warrior."

"We will speak of this," Jerd said, and he sank to the ground.

"Yes, we will speak of it," Namacho said. "But first, there is another matter to which I must attend. As we were riding, far east of here, we saw the buzzards. They circled their prey, but were frightened away. It was because of you, my brother, that the buzzards fled."

Jerd frowned, but nodded.

"We came to the place where the buzzards would have feasted, had you not come. We read the signs in the sand. We found the cairn of stones beneath which you buried one of our people. His ears had been stolen."

Jerd could guess what was coming next. Namacho and many other Apaches knew of the grisly trophies Clem Driggs collected. Undoubtedly, Driggs had been recognized.

Namacho smiled. "It was when I saw the Ear-robber,

and saw that he was bound, that I knew you were still my brother. What would you have done with him?"

"I had not decided," Jerd answered.

"The ghosts of those he has murdered cry to the sky for justice. Before the moon arises, their cries will be stilled. Give him to us, my brother."

"His own people will punish him."

Namacho showed a flash of anger. "They will do nothing. We will deal with the Ear-robber in our own way."

"No."

Namacho spoke again, his voice lower but still showing a trace of anger. "You are not making it easier for me. Many of us do not remember you. Is it your wish to die with the Ear-robber?"

Jerd was standing again. He stared bleakly at Driggs, realizing there was no way he could save him. If he persisted in trying, it would cost his own life. The way things stood he might not escape anyhow. Only the whim of Namacho could save him. As for Driggs, if Jerd was honest, the man richly deserved what lay ahead. In what he had done this morning—in the shooting of the old Indian in the back—Jerd had a sample of Driggs' past life. Driggs was a white man, surely, but not one of whom Jerd could be proud.

Jerd looked away and his words were brittle. "It will be as you wish, my brother. The Ear-robber is yours."

Namacho swung away. He gave an order, and three of his braves moved toward Driggs. Until now Driggs had been silent, terrified, shocked at what had happened. But now he started screaming. He was still screaming as the Indians reached him and jerked him erect.

His screaming would continue for a long time.

The sun finally went down. Darkness crept over the land. As it grew deeper it hid the figure of the man who had once been Clem Driggs. He still lived, but not consciously. His ears were gone, his face was unrecognizable, his body was laced with torturing cuts. Witnessing what had happened to him hadn't been easy on Jerd. He was revolted at such practises, but he had to hide it, and as well as he could, he did.

Turning away from the others, Namacho walked to

where Jerd was sitting. It was too dark to see the Indian's eyes, but his voice was caustic. "You did not join us, my brother. Perhaps your blood has turned thin?"

"Would you test it, Namacho?" Jerd challenged.

"Then ride with us. You will be tested, soon enough. Did you not recently live in the Canyon of the Buzzards?"

"Our people call it Eden."

"Our name was better. In two nights, those who are living there will be dead. The buzzards will pick their bones."

Nearby several of the Indians were building a supper fire. Jerd glanced that way, but he noticed them only vaguely. What Namacho had said made him uneasy. Eden canyon, far south of here and deep in the barrens, was a phenomenon—a rich and lush land isolated in the surrounding desert—a wide canyon, well watered, and now settled by half a dozen families. He had been one of the first to settle there, for in the beginning, the threat of Indian trouble had discouraged people from trying it. Then others had moved in, among them, one Sam Rogell. Right now Jerd didn't care much what happened to Rogell, but as for the others—

He looked at Namacho. "I was told you would do nothing until you had heard from the Mimbres."

"They are old women," Namacho said scornfully.

"I have heard the general would like to see you."

"He speaks in many tongues. I have no wish to see him—unless it is to see him over the sights of my rifle."

"He can send many men against you, my brother."

The Indian shrugged. "Each of us must die. I do not wish to live, cowering in my lodge, blanketed by fear. It is more honorable to die as a warrior. How will it be with you?"

Jerd picked his words carefully. "I could live in your lodge, and with great pleasure. I could ride with you on a hunt as we did long ago. But to turn against the people with whom I have lived is a grave matter. I would like more time. We will speak of this again in the morning."

Namacho made an angry motion with his arm. "I do not like this. If you had not been my brother and if you had not made a prisoner of the Ear-robber, you would have died."

"Then do as you wish."

"It was my plan to ride on, when the moon comes up."

"If that is to happen, you must ride without me."

"You have chosen to die."

"Then let it be your hand to strike the blow."

Namacho swung away. He marched to the fire and stood there, his back to Jerd. What was in the Indian's mind, Jerd couldn't guess. He knew that his life hung by a thread. He had hoped to delay his decision through the night just on the chance that he might be able to escape before morning. But Namacho didn't want to stay here. He wanted to ride on. In two hours the moon would be up. Jerd might have that much margin. Or he might not. At any moment Namacho might decide he couldn't be trusted.

Jerd sat where he was, a huddled, motionless figure on the ground. He still had his holster gun and his knife, but he knew that with the Indians all around, he couldn't do very much if it came to a struggle. He also knew where his horse was tied and where the Indians' horses were located, but to reach a horse and escape looked impossible. Right now, no one seemed to be paying any attention to him. If he moved, however, every Indian in the camp would be watching him.

The Indians had their supper. No one offered any food to him, nor did Jerd move to the fire. He sweated through the next hour, and hoped that from his attitude, he seemed lost in thought. Some of the Indians rolled on their blankets and stretched out on the ground to rest. Others sat around the fire, some silent, some talking, Namacho among them. He was at the side, squatting on the earth where he could glance at Jerd. Driggs had been neglected, but perhaps he was dead and of no more interest to them.

Another hour passed. The moon came up, a nearly full moon. Down in the rolling barrens the white desert sands seemed to glisten under the golden sheen of the moon's brightness, and even under the trees the shadows crept back closer to the ground.

Namacho stood up. He gave several gruff orders, then

turned and walked toward Jerd and his words were harsh. "Well, my brother, have you chosen?"

Jerd raised his head. "It is not morning. I am no child to be hurried."

"We have many miles to cover. We cannot wait until morning."

Jerd spoke again. "Among the people with whom I have lived are some I could ride against as an Apache. But with them is another—a woman. Her hair is like gold and her face is as fair as the morning. I would not like to see her harmed. When the sun arises in the east, I will have made my decision."

Namacho fingered his knife. He seemed troubled. "Your skin is white, but I have still called you my brother. I think you are against us, yet I do not know how you stand. I, Namacho of the Chiricahua Apaches, try to be a fair man. Because of this I will give you until morning to make your decision."

"You are truly a chief, my brother."

"It will be like this," Namacho said. "Two of our people will stay behind, until morning. As the sun comes up, you will announce your decision. If you are to ride with us, they will bring you to my side. If you are to be against us, you will be killed."

"I cannot quarrel with that."

"Farewell, my brother."

"Farewell."

Namacho twisted away. He shouted an order. One of the Indians, already mounted, wheeled past leading Namacho's horse. Namacho grasped the horse's mane and swung up. Then, in the matter of less than a minute, Jerd heard the fading hoofbeats of the Indians' horses. From what he could see, everyone had left. But Namacho had said two Indians would be left behind—and he wouldn't have forgotten them. Because of that, Jerd still sat where he was, motionless, and apparently deep in thought.

The moon climbed higher and turned silver. The fire burned to embers, and finally went out. Around where Jerd was sitting, nothing moved. Deeper in the trees, his horse might have been standing, and at some other point, two other horses might be tied. The Indians' horses. And definitely, somewhere in the scanty shadows, two of the

Indians were watching him. Jerd had to count on that.

It was a long night. There was no way to hurry the hours. He had set sunup as the hour to make his decision. If he moved earlier, the Indians watching him would be suspicious. As an Apache, he would have held to his pledge—and if he expected to live he couldn't step out of his role until the last definitive moment.

Jerd had forgotten the sheriff back in Wickenburg and the posse which had chased him. He forgot about Clem Driggs whose death had shaken him. In the days ahead he might remember his screaming, and shudder, but under the circumstances, he couldn't have helped him. Instead of worrying about Driggs, or his own problems, Jerd spent a little time speculating on Namacho's campaign.

After fleeing the reservation with a number of young braves, Namacho had done a traditional thing in leading his men in a raid below the border. Other chiefs, in other outbreaks of trouble, had done the same thing —made a raid into Mexico. This was a test of strength, and a training expedition. The long riding, the camping, the fighting hardened the young men and turned them into veterans. They learned to go on short rations, to go without water or rest. They learned to fight, to burn, and to kill—for even an Indian had to learn to be a warrior.

Those whom Namacho led into Mexico had returned as seasoned fighters. The soldiers who went after them wouldn't have an easy time, for Namacho's band, in all probability, would be able to hit at one point and, by the next morning after a full day's ride, be fifty miles away. Namacho knew the area, too. He wouldn't be trapped easily.

Looking at the entire picture, one factor puzzled Jerd. Following the successful raid into Mexico, it was hard to understand why some Mimbres hadn't joined Namacho. Magnas Coloradas, their chief, he knew was a dominant leader. He had signed a peace treaty, just as had Cochise. But among the Mimbres, just as among the Chiricahuas, there were numerous young men, hot-blooded, excitable. It seemed strange that some of these younger Mimbres hadn't cast their lot with Namacho.

Jerd shifted position, but only to relax his cramped

muscles. He took another slow, sweeping look from side to side. An hour ago, he thought he had located the hiding place of one of the Indians, but he wasn't sure. He had no idea where the second Indian was concealed.

Scowling, Jerd stared at the dead fire, abruptly remembering Namacho's immediate plans—to head for Eden canyon. If nothing interfered, his band would hit the settlement with the next dawn—twenty-seven hours from now. Jerd had hoped that if he could get away, he would be able to warn the people in the canyon, but as things stood now, he wasn't sure he could make it in time. And he hadn't yet escaped. What would happen in the morning was problematic.

It wasn't a pleasant thing to consider what might happen to the people in Eden canyon, if he didn't get there ahead of the Indians. Sam Rogell lived there. He had said he didn't care what happened to Rogell, but that wasn't quite true. He didn't want the man killed. At least not yet. In his own opinion, Sam Rogell knew the secret of the stage holdup, for which Jerd had been arrested.

And he was worried about Laurie Hale, who lived in the canyon with her parents. He and Laurie had been planning to be married. Of course, since his arrest and conviction, he didn't rate very high with Laurie's father and mother. But he never had. Laurie, however, had stood by him. A brave, stubborn girl. Damnit, he had to get to the canyon before tomorrow morning.

Of course, some of those in the canyon might have fled, might have moved to Wickenburg, or some other safe place. But not everyone. Since Namacho had returned, he had made no raids in the Territory. His name was a threat, but without real substance. People were alarmed, but not yet frightened. Because of that, in all probability, most of the settlers in Eden canyon would still be there.

Jerd looked up at the moon and then stared toward the east. The sky held a soft light, faintly brighter above the distant Sierra Robles. The night was passing. In another hour dawn would be breaking. In another hour . . .

The minutes slid by. It grew noticeably brighter. Jerd finally got to his feet. He turned to face the east and, raising his arms, stood holding them toward the sunrise. It was years since he had lived as an Apache. He had forgotten many of the customs, many of the rituals. What significance the two watching Indians would see in what he was doing, he didn't know, but he wanted to seem reverent and wholly untroubled. Apparently he had spent the night in thoughtful deliberation. He would play the same role for a little longer.

Jerd sat down again. After a time one of the Indians stepped in sight from behind a screen of shrubbery and walked toward him. He carried a rifle, and looked ready to use it. Jerd didn't look up at the man.

The Indian motioned vaguely to the east. "You have greeted the morning. What do you have to tell me?"

"We will ride to meet my brother, Namacho," Jerd answered. "I, Tajawan, am one of the Chiricahuas. I have returned to my people."

"Tajawan?"

"So I was called in my youth."

The Indian seemed to have relaxed. "It will be a long ride to join the others. We should lose no more time."

"Then we will start at once," Jerd said.

He got to his feet, stretched and flexed his muscles, and after that, walked in the direction of his horse. He showed no concern at all, but a driving question was gnawing at his mind. *Where was the second Indian?* Until they were both in sight he had to act as an Apache.

He reached his horse, spent a little time examining it, delaying until he heard the Indian coming back. He had gone after his horse and he seemed suspicious that Jerd wasn't ready.

"What is it now, Tajawan?" he asked sharply.

"It is this bruise which worries me," Jerd said, pointing to one of the forefeet of his horse.

The Indian rode closer. He stared down, but didn't dismount. And for that, Jerd was thankful. There was nothing wrong with his horse.

"An Apache cares for his horse," the Indian muttered.

"I was occupied by the Ear-robber. Have you no other horses?"

"No."

Jerd stooped over, still seemingly worried about his horse. *But where was the second Indian?* He would ride in sight, undoubtedly, as they left, but if one rode in front of him, and one behind, he would be in an unenviable position.

The first Indian solved the problem for him. Twisting away, he shouted, "Chalana! Chalana, take a look at Tajawan's horse."

The second Indian came in sight through the trees, a thin, round-shouldered man, nearing his thirties. He rode closer, reined up, slipped to the ground and approached Jerd's horse. Stooping over, he ran his hands over the horse's legs.

Jerd didn't wait for the man's verdict. He stepped to one side, whipped up his holster gun. The mounted Indian saw the motion. He uttered a short cry of warning and tried to use his rifle. He nearly managed it, but Jerd's shot came too fast. It hit the Indian squarely in the chest, lifted him backwards. As he was falling, Jerd swung on the second.

That warning cry had startled the second Indian. He drove straight at Jerd, one arm extended, his other hand reaching for his knife. Jerd tried to get his gun down, but he wasn't in time. The thrust of the Indian's arm knocked him off balance. He reeled away, stumbled to the ground, and as he went down the Indian sprawled half across him, his knife arm now slashing at Jerd. Jerd twisted his gun, fired, and blocked the stabbing knife. He fired again, and this second bullet was enough. The Indian shuddered, and collapsed.

Jerd rolled the Indian away. He sat up, breathing heavily. Then he got to his feet, mopped his hand across his face, and looked to where the first Indian had fallen. He wasn't moving. Possibly he was dead. Jerd made sure of it, and after that took another look at the second Indian. Chalana, as he had been called, still was living. But he wouldn't last very long. He wouldn't recover consciousness.

The Indians' horses had danced away, and Jerd's was pulling at his tether, excited by the gunfire. Jerd moved that way. He patted the horse reassuringly, took a look from side to side. Yesterday morning he had found an old Indian, lying dead. He had taken the time to build a rock cairn over his body. This time he couldn't, nor could he worry about Clem Driggs. It was a long ride to Eden canyon. He didn't have a minute to waste. To the east, the sun was just coming up over the Sierra Robles.

Chapter III

MIDGE APPLEGATE AWOKE suddenly. She rose on her elbow and looked toward the window. She felt startled, frightened, but she didn't know why. Something had aroused her, but she didn't know what. She remembered no sounds which might have stirred her, and certainly, right now, nothing was wrong. The window was a grey oblong, brighter than when she had gone to bed. The sky was lighter, an indication morning was near.

She took a deep, steadying breath. That helped, but her body was still tense. It ran through her mind that they might have to face an Indian attack. Such a possibility didn't make her feel any better. Some Indian chief, she forgot his name, had led a band of warriors into Mexico, but then had returned and taken refuge in the Sierra Robles. It was rumored that he was trying to excite the entire Apache nation, and if that happened, there might be trouble everywhere in the Territory.

Her uncle, Dan Hale, didn't think the trouble would go that far. Cochise and Magnas Coloradas, the two most important Indian chiefs in the Territory, had reassured the authorities of their peaceful intentions. If they held firm, the renegade Indians in the Sierra Robles wouldn't last very long. A punitive expedition would be sent after them and would trap them. But of course, there might be some trouble. Her uncle admitted such a possibility.

The other figure in the bed turned restlessly, but didn't awaken. Midge glanced at her. Laurie Hale, her bed companion and her cousin, lay far at the edge, as though withdrawn. That, Midge decided, was a good characterization of their relationship. When she had moved here two months before, Laurie had welcomed her. But she didn't really like her, or like sharing her bed. There had been no trouble between them, of course, and there wouldn't be. Laurie was too much a lady.

Midge sighed. She slipped out of bed and walked to the window. There was a chill in the morning air which made her shiver, and it was hard to realize that by ten o'clock it would be quite hot. That was one of the strange, conflicting things about this country. There were others. This canyon was a beautifully green place, but all around was the desert. The men she had met seemed friendly, yet they carried guns and not only against the Indians. It seemed as though she had moved into a different world.

She was right. The sky was growing lighter. From the window she could see her uncle's barn quite clearly, the adjoining haystack, and the green fields beyond where the corn was already high, some of it topping.

A figure appeared suddenly at the edge of the cornfield. *An Indian!* Midge raised her hands to her throat. She could feel the scream building up there, but before she could let it out she realized the figure wasn't an Indian. Or at least, she didn't think it was an Indian. The man wore buckskins and a wide-brimmed hat. He was carrying a rifle and he seemed hurt. As he moved forward he staggered and fell. But then he got up and staggered on. In another moment he disappeared behind the haystack.

Midge stood motionless at the window, not quite sure what to do. If the man was hurt, undoubtedly she ought to call her uncle. He was in another room but she could wake Laurie and Laurie could arouse him without raising a commotion.

She turned to the bed, touched Laurie's shoulder, and then shook her. She spoke in a loud whisper. "Laurie, Laurie—wake up. There's someone outside."

"Go back to sleep," Laurie said sleepily. "It's the middle of the night."

"It's nearly morning—and I did see someone outside. A man. I think he's been hurt."

Laurie sat up. Something in Midge's voice startled her. She looked toward the window, her lips working. A hoarse word came from her throat. "Indians!" Then she spoke again, raising her voice to a shout. "Indians! Indians! Indians!"

"It wasn't an Indian," Midge said. "At least, I don't think it was an Indian."

She walked back to the window, looked outside. The man she had seen had rounded the haystack and was weaving uncertainly toward the house—a tall, thin man, limping, trailing his rifle.

Her uncle's voice spoke from the bedroom door behind her, and he sounded excited. "Midge, get away from that window. If any of them red savages . . ."

"It's not an Indian," Midge answered. "It's a white man. I'm sure of it."

Dan Hale crossed the room to join her. He wore a knee-length nightgown and was barefooted. His iron-grey hair was mussed from the pillow. He was a gaunt, bony man, tall and round-shouldered, sharp-featured. He was gripping his rifle.

Midge pointed into the yard. "He's almost here."

Hale had raised his rifle but, as he peered through the window, he lowered it. He muttered a name. "Jerd Galway!"

"Jerd!" Laurie gasped.

"I won't stand for it," Hale said. "How did he have the nerve to show up here! We'll send him packing."

Laurie spoke again. "But, father . . ."

Hale turned to look at her. His voice was gruff. "I thought you had got over your foolishness about him. You know what he's done. He's a convicted holdup man. A fugitive from justice. What we should do is hold him for the sheriff."

Laurie bit her lips. "No, father. I wish . . ."

"You stay in your bed," Hale ordered. "I'll handle him. I don't want you to see him."

He left the room, closed the door.

Midge looked at Laurie. She had swung her feet to the floor, was sitting on the edge of the bed, and in the half-light seeping through the window she looked frightened, confused. Midge stared at her thoughtfully. She knew, vaguely, the details of Jerd Galway's arrest and conviction. She knew that Jerd had once lived here in

Eden canyon, and had heard he was in love with Laurie. But she and her cousin hadn't been close. They had never talked about him. How Laurie actually felt about him, Midge didn't know. If she had to guess she would say that Laurie had made a good recovery. At least, recently, she had devoted considerable attention to Sam Rogell, and if she missed Jerd Galway, she didn't show it. Sam was an older man—at least forty. He wasn't unattractive, but Midge didn't like him at all.

"What am I going to do?" Laurie asked, looking toward her.

"That's easy," Midge replied. "If you don't want to see the man, stay in bed. Or, if you do want to see him, get dressed and walk into the next room. That's what I'm going to do."

"It's not that simple," Laurie answered. "Once, Jerd and I . . ."

She didn't finish. Tears flooded her eyes and she twisted away and buried her face in her pillow.

"I'm getting dressed," Midge said.

She slipped out of her nightgown, reached for her clothes. She was slender, tall, dark-haired, and just past nineteen. She didn't look strong, but she could spend a full day in the fields, keeping up with Dan Hale. She had a wiry strength which didn't show. Her eyes were dark, steady, and she could laugh easily.

Voices from the next room came through the door, harsh, angry voices, but what the men were saying wasn't clear. Midge finished dressing, glanced at Laurie who hadn't moved, then headed for the parlor. It wouldn't be light for another hour but it wasn't too dark to see Dan Hale and the man who had just arrived. He had dropped on a sofa. Her uncle was standing over him.

"Indians? I don't believe a word of it," Hale said.

The man on the sofa seemed tired. "You'd better believe it."

"Namacho's in the Sierra Robles. His band was cut to pieces in Mexico. Maybe there's still a few of them left, and he might round up some more, but the last we heard, the army's after him."

"Sure, the army will get him—but not right away."

Hale moved to the window, peered outside. He shook his head. "Don't see anyone out there."

"Of course you don't. And you won't see anyone until it's lighter. We've got maybe an hour. Ring your signal bell, Dan. Don't be a damned fool."

"If it was anyone else . . ."

The man on the sofa straightened. "Damnit, man, use your head for a change. Sure I was arrested and convicted of a holdup, but that doesn't have anything to do with this. I've been out in the barrens and up in the Mesquite hills. Indian country. I've lived with the Indians, and know them. Who would know better what to expect of them? If there's any chance in the world they might hit us this morning, use your signal bell. Warn the others."

Midge could feel a pounding excitement. It didn't occur to her to question what the man had said. An Indian attack was imminent. On a hundred occasions during the past weeks she had wondered what it would be like if she had to face such an experience. Some of the stories she had heard about Indian attacks were blood-curdling. It was suddenly hard to breathe.

"Who's that?" the man on the sofa asked, looking toward her. "Laurie . . ."

"I'm Midge Applegate, her cousin," Midge said. "Laurie isn't up yet."

Hale glanced at her. "Ask her to get dressed. And knock on my door, tell my wife to get up. I'm going to ring the signal bell. But if this is a scheme . . ."

"It is," Jerd said. "It's a scheme to give you a chance to fight back."

Mrs. Hale was already up, and was dressing. So was Laurie. She was putting on a freshly ironed dress, one which she ordinarily wouldn't have used until afternoon when Sam Rogell might drop by. Her hair had been done, too. Midge's was still in braids.

"What did he say?" Laurie asked. "Did father . . ."

She broke off, stiffened, and caught her breath as the bell in the short tower outside started ringing. She whispered, "Oh, no. Not that!"

The bell continued ringing. To Midge, it didn't sound terribly loud, but she had been told that the sounds would

carry up and down the canyon, and to every other
house. And some of the others also had warning bells.

Laurie looked at her. "Did Jerd really say that the
Indians . . ."

"That's what he said," Midge nodded. "In about an
hour—at dawn. What does that mean?"

"The others in the valley will come here if they have
time. At least, Sam will make it. And when Sam and
Jerd face each other . . ."

"You mean they don't get along?"

"Jerd blames Sam for what happened. He insists he
was innocent. He thinks the holdup was—was arranged,
just to get him in trouble, so Sam could get Jerd's land
in the lower canyon."

"Did he?" Midge asked bluntly.

"Certainly not. At least, Sam had nothing to do with
the holdup. And if he filed a claim on Jerd's land, why
that was just a business matter. Someone else would have
claimed the land. There's no reason Sam shouldn't have
done it."

"What about you?"

Laurie frowned. "You ask too many questions. Fix
your hair."

"No one cares about my hair," Midge said. "Unless it's
the Indians."

"That's not being funny," Laurie said sharply. "An
Indian attack is no joke. I just wish we had moved to
Wickenburg. We'd have been safe if we had."

The bell continued tolling. Its clear notes in the
grey of the morning made a shiver run down Midge's
back. She knew that an Indian attack was no joke. She
hadn't been trying to be funny. Inside, she was quite
shaky. Just to be doing something, she started fixing her
hair.

"Let me help you," Laurie said.

She had never offered to do that before. And in all
probability, Midge realized, Laurie wasn't interested in
helping her now. But it postponed the moment when
she would have to face Jerd Galway, in the next room.
It gave her more time to think, to brace herself.

Midge stared thoughtfully at the window. They were in
peril of an Indian attack. In view of that, they should

be thinking of nothing else. But Laurie had another matter on her mind. And if Jerd Galway and Sam Rogell hated each other, both would bear watching. The morning, just ahead, might be explosive.

Jerd listened to the tolling of the bell. He smiled, then spoke half aloud. "Are you listening, Namacho? How do you like it? Too bad your attack won't be a surprise."

He could picture the Indians somewhere in the trees along the river. They would have been startled by the warning bell. They wouldn't like what had happened. To the Indians, surprise was half of the battle.

Jerd shifted position. Every muscle in his body seemed in protest against the punishment he had taken in getting here. He had ridden almost without rest until his horse gave out. After that he had traveled by foot, at a steady dog-trot. As a youth with the Apaches, he could have run all night and not felt it. But his legs weren't what they once had been. Sitting now on the sofa, he wasn't sure he could get up. He was hungry, too, but that could wait.

The bell outside stopped tolling, and as he listened he heard answers from down the canyon, and up. They were signals that help was coming. In the next few minutes, if things worked out as planned, every family in the canyon would be on their way to Dan Hale's. If there was no delay, most should get here in the next half-hour, well before dawn. A dozen men and women and several nearly grown children, all well armed. With a force like that, they could make a good defense. Namacho wasn't going to have an easy victory.

Mrs. Hale appeared from one of the bedrooms. She looked at him uncertainly, then moved to the stove and started a fire. Her husband came inside. He crossed to the stove to talk to her, then he swung toward Jerd. "I just hope you know what you're doing," he said heavily. "If we've called everyone here—just for nothing . . ."

"It wasn't for nothing," Jerd said.

"I never saw it more quiet outside."

"Then if it stays quiet, we're lucky. While you've got

a chance, you ought to carry more water inside from the well."

"I know what to do," Dan said sourly.

The two girls appeared from the other bedroom. Laurie, and the girl he had seen earlier. They were nearly of the same size and in the darkness of the room, Jerd couldn't decide which was which. But after a brief hesitation, one walked toward him and as she drew nearer Jerd recognized Laurie.

She spoke his name uncertainly. "Jerd?"

"Hello, Laurie," Jerd answered.

He wanted to say more. He wanted to stretch out his hands toward her. He wanted to tell her how much it had meant to him to know she hadn't believed him guilty of the holdup. But perhaps he would have the time to say that later.

She spoke again. "Midge saw you through the window. She thought you were hurt."

"I'm just tired," Jerd said. "If I stumbled, it was because my legs wouldn't work any longer. I'll be all right in a few minutes."

Hale interrupted them, his words harsh. "Laurie, help your mother."

She hesitated, frowning, but then said, "Yes, father." And turned away to walk toward the stove.

From outside, Jerd heard the sound of driving hoof-beats pulling into the yard—several horses bringing Hale's nearest neighbors. Then, from the other direction, more horses.

"I'll see who's coming," Hale said, and he headed for the door.

Jerd leaned back on the sofa. It seemed a little lighter. Both girls, now, were helping Mrs. Hale, setting out plates and cups or working at the stove. The one he had just met, Midge Applegate, had dark hair in contrast to Laurie's blondness. She had quick, sure movements. He still couldn't see her face clearly but he liked the way she held her head, the square set of her shoulders, and her erect carriage. He guessed the girls were about the same age.

But he spent only a moment thinking about Midge.

Laurie concerned him much more. Dan Hale never had approved Jerd's interest in Laurie, and since his arrest, without much question Hale's antagonism had deepened. In view of her father's attitude, it was an encouraging thing that Laurie had the courage to speak to him.

He heard voices on the porch outside, and a moment later, Lou Carling came in with his wife and baby, followed by the Ellsworths, a man and wife and two nearly grown children. The women and children moved deeper into the room but the men stopped near the sofa and looked uneasily at Jerd.

" 'Morning, Ellsworth—Carling," Jerd said. "I wish I could have brought better news."

Carling scrubbed his jaw. He was short, wide-shouldered, heavy, and about forty years old. "Heard you got away from the sheriff," he said slowly. "As we got it, the posse chased you into the barrens, almost to the Sierra Robles."

"Yes, they did," Jerd admitted.

"Reckon that's how come you ran into the 'Paches."

"I suppose it is."

"Used to live with 'em, didn't you?"

"Long ago."

Ellsworth had something to ask. He edged forward and said, "Hale mentioned Namacho. Last word we had, Namacho was in the Sierra Robles."

"He didn't stay there," Jerd said. "I met him in the Mesquite hills, almost due north of here."

"How come he let you go?"

"He didn't exactly. I'll tell you the full story later. Right now, the point is this. Namacho will hit us this morning, probably at dawn. He didn't have many braves with him when I saw him, but that's no promise he won't have more."

Some others had ridden into the yard. Footsteps pounded across the porch, the door opened, and Sam Rogell stepped inside. He was followed by the three men who worked for him, Mike Foss, Joe Ingraham and Bern Vanderveer. But Jerd was only vaguely aware of them. He centered his attention on Rogell.

No one was outside to tell Rogell whom he would meet. It must have come to him as a shocking surprise to find Jerd Galway. It was growing lighter in the room, light enough so Jerd could see the man's face, a rugged, handsome face, square-jawed, strong. He had wide-spaced grey eyes, a straight nose, tight, thin lips. On his upper lip was a bristling, black mustache. Sam Rogell had a hearty laugh and he could smile charmingly, but he wasn't showing his smile this morning. His features had hardened; his eyes were like granite.

He stared at Jerd for perhaps ten seconds, then, with a smoothness which was startling, he whipped up his holster gun, leveled it, and grated out a question. "Where the hell did you come from?"

"Up north. The Mesquite hills," Jerd answered.

A scowl had gathered on Rogell's forehead. "Hale, this why you rang the bell?"

"No. Injuns," Hale said. "Galway says they're coming."

"No one would know better than him," Rogell said, and there was a veiled suggestion in his words. He was still staring at Jerd. He hadn't lowered his gun. He spoke again. "When they gonna hit us?"

"Probably at dawn," Jerd said.

"Namacho?"

"Yes."

"How many with him?"

"I don't know."

Rogell was silent for a moment, possibly weighing what Jerd had said. Then he spoke, almost to himself. "Looks like we'll get burned out, every place but here. Hell with the 'Paches. We ought to wipe 'em out, to the last man. Never be safe until we do."

"I feel just like you do," Lou Carling said.

Rogell nodded. "We'll do it, too, but in the meantime we're facing a little trouble right in our own camp. Galway, I'll take your gun."

Jerd didn't reach for his gun. He didn't move except to shake his head. "Sorry, Rogell. We're facing an Indian attack. To turn it back, we'll need every man we've got."

"We don't need your kind."

Jerd's answer was mild. "I can handle a gun, Rogell. In fact, I'm rather good. If Namacho's got a crowd with him, you'll need me."

Rogell pushed his head forward aggressively. "After this is over, you're going back to the sheriff."

"Why don't we let that go until later?"

"By God, we're gonna decide it now."

Jerd straightened, and shook his head. "Drop it, Rogell. We're going to have our hands full, living through the morning. If we make it, then turn me over to the sheriff —if you can."

He shouldn't have added those last three words, and he knew it. Several of the men standing around them stiffened, and didn't like it. But they were interrupted by the arrival of the Dawsons, and by John Boulder, who had turned to the window to look outside.

"Hey, I just saw one of 'em, at the corner of the barn," he shouted.

Seth Dawson, still in the doorway, gave a gasp, then he lurched forward and pitched to the floor. As he fell, his wife screamed, then dropped at his side. Deeply buried in his back, between his shoulderblades, was the feathered shaft of an arrow. The Indians were here, just outside. The attack was under way.

Chapter IV

THE INDIANS HURLED themselves directly at the house, racing their horses, and making the morning horrible with sound. As they neared the building they veered to the side and swept past it, screaming, yelling, hurling spears and using bow and arrow, a few firing their rifles. From beyond the house they circled back, this time splitting into two groups to pass both sides of the structure. Then, hardly taking time to regroup themselves, they came again.

Jerd moved to one of the side windows. He fired carefully at the bobbing figures which raced past. But it was still grey, not fully light, and his aiming had to be almost instinctive. Even when the sky grew brighter, hitting a moving target wouldn't be easy, and the Indians, hugging their horses and riding half out of sight on the far sides, didn't give them much to shoot at.

This type of attack was more clever than most people would admit. He had heard dozens of men discount the Indians as effective warriors. Their wild shooting from the backs of their horses seldom hit one of the defenders and their screaming didn't kill anyone. That was true, but too many forgot the wasted shots the defenders threw away and, if the siege lasted very long, the matter of ammunition became very important. Many a cabin might have been defended successfully if those inside hadn't run out of bullets.

Considering that, Jerd stopped firing. He glanced around, scanning the interior of the main room. Dan Hale had built a rather substantial house. It was of log construction, well chinked and paneled inside. It was square and had four rooms, two bedrooms and a storage room on the north, and one large general room with windows on three sides. The east part of the room held the kitchen, a stove, two tables, several chairs and the inevitable alcoves. The remainder of the room could have been considered the parlor.

On the east and west were two doors, each flanked by a window. On the south wall were three windows. Jerd was at one of those side windows, the one toward the front. With him, at the other corner, was Bern Vanderveer who worked for Rogell. Aaron Ellsworth and his son Erb were at the next. Erb was about fourteen. George Odlum, one of the last to arrive, and his wife were at the third side window, John Boulder, Mike Foss, and two people Jerd didn't immediately identify were at the rear windows. Carling and Dan Hale were at the front windows. Several of the women were on the floor. Jerd didn't see Rogell, Laurie, Joe Ingraham or Midge Applegate, but they might have been defending the bedroom windows. Seth Dawson had been carried to one of those rooms. His wife probably was with him but without much question he was dead.

Jerd set his rifle aside. He rolled and lit a cigarette. As he lit it, Vanderveer spoke. "Grab your rifle. Here they come again."

"What of it?" Jerd asked. "How many of them have you hit?"

"By God, whose side are you on?"

"Let me put it this way," Jerd said. "How many shells have you got?"

"A pocketful."

"If you fire them as fast as you can, how many will be left in another hour? How many will be left by noon, if the fight goes on?"

Vanderveer pushed back his hat. He was freckled, hawk-faced, about thirty. He squinted thoughtfully and in a moment he nodded. "Maybe you got somethin' there. Shootin' at the varmints right now is like shootin' at ghosts."

Outside, the Apaches wheeled past, screaming and yelling, firing their rifles and arrows, a few hurling spears. They circled beyond the house and swept by again. After this flurry of action, Vanderveer got up, hurried across the room, and disappeared in one of the bedrooms. A moment later he came in sight once more, this time following Sam Rogell.

"Listen to me—all of you," Rogell shouted, making the words a command. "Cut down on your firing. Save your bullets for later. This fight might last all day."

Several people looked around at him but no one answered directly.

Rogell spoke again. "Cut down on your shooting—everyone."

Jerd wasn't surprised at Rogell's assumption of authority. From what he knew of the man, Rogell liked to run things. His aggressive attitude wasn't something put on.

Dan Hale left the front of the room, walked toward Rogell, spoke to him for a moment, then headed for Jerd. Rogell and Vanderveer followed him.

"I've never been caught in an Indian attack," Hale said. "Maybe you know what's ahead."

"I could guess," Jerd nodded.

"No one can guess what the 'Paches will do," Rogell said sharply.

"That's true enough," Jerd agreed. "But there are a few things we can figure on. From the way things have started, I think the Indians will make a few more passes at the house. If we cut down on our shooting, they'll figure we are short on ammunition, or maybe some of us have been hurt, so they'll rush the windows."

"You mean, we shouldn't cut down on our shooting?" Hale asked.

"No, we've got to save our ammunition," Jerd said. "We've got to save it against the time when they try to bust in. That's bound to happen."

"What will happen if we hold the windows?"

"They may try to bust in again or they might try to burn us out—set the roof on fire."

"Blazing arrows?"

"Probably."

"Had a hard rain yesterday. Roof must still be wet. Not much wind to help whip up a blaze."

"Then we're in luck."

Hale ruffed his hand through his hair. "Suppose we hold the house? How long will the Indians press the attack?"

Jerd shook his head. "Hale, I don't know. Namacho might keep his people here all day and tomorrow, too. There's no way to tell what to expect. I think Namacho expected an easy time, here in Eden canyon. Maybe he's working on a schedule and wants to get somewhere tomorrow. Or he might be in no hurry at all."

The Indians whirled past the house again, Hale, Rogell and Vanderveer crouching to the floor as they raced by. Only a few of the defenders fired back. The Indians circled and came by once more. This time they rode closer to the house.

"Another time or two, and they'll be hitting the windows," Jerd said. "Tell your men not to fire again until we see the Indians trying to climb in. Then don't miss."

Hale nodded soberly. "I'll pass the word to the others."

He started around the room, from window to window. Vanderveer got down, and Sam Rogell, crouching nearby, glared steadily at Jerd.

"Something on your mind, Rogell?" Jerd asked.

"You're damned right," Rogell answered. "I'm getting an idea I don't like. It's a pretty ugly thing. You used to live with the 'Paches, didn't you?"

"That's right."

"Blood-brother to Namacho, ain't you?"

"That was long ago."

"Yeah? Maybe so—or maybe not. Could be you brought the Injuns here."

"You'd like to prove that, wouldn't you?"

"Maybe I will."

"How will you go about it?" Jerd asked. "Find a renegade who's been kicked out of his tribe? Maybe with a bottle of whiskey, you could buy him."

Rogell shook his head. "I'll get at the truth, Galway. That's a promise."

Off to the side, holding two cups of coffee, was Midge Applegate. Before the previous attack he had noticed her, carrying coffee to some of the men at the rear of the room. Now, before the next charge, she was serving others. As he looked up at her he saw the shocked expression in her eyes. What she thought, or how much she had heard, he couldn't guess.

"That coffee for me?" Rogell asked, reaching out. "Thanks, Midge."

The girl handed him one of the cups, hesitated, then extended the other toward Jerd.

He accepted it, smiling, and said, "Thanks, I need this."

"I'll bring another to Mr. Vanderveer," Midge said.

"Put a shot of whiskey in it," Vanderveer drawled.

"I'm afraid I don't have any," Midge said.

Jerd could hear the Indians hurling forward and he motioned to the girl. "Get down. Some of those arrows hit the windows."

"I'm going back to where I was," Rogell said. "But I ain't forgetting what I said. If I'm right about what I think, Galway, you'll never last long enough to get back to jail."

He jerked erect, then pounded across the room toward one of the bedrooms.

Midge, nearby, crouched to the floor. She stared at the windows while the Indians screamed by. After they were gone, Jerd took a quick look outside. It was fully light by now. In a few more minutes, the sun would be up.

"I'll get your coffee now, Mr. Vanderveer," Midge said.

The man shook his head. "Nope, they'll be back. You stay where you're put. Those varmints make two passes, then they take a breath. That's when to go after coffee."

Jerd nodded, and glanced at the girl. "He's right, Midge."

She was frowning, and what she said surprised him. "Why didn't you talk back to him?"

"You mean Rogell?"

"Yes. If what he said wasn't true, why didn't you answer him? Or was he right? Is that why you were silent?"

"No, he wasn't right," Jerd answered. "But this isn't the time to fight him. We've got an Indian attack on our hands. That comes first."

The Indians streamed by again. Midge hugged the floor, then after they were gone she got up and hurried toward the stove.

"Never noticed her before very much," Vanderveer said. "Seen her only with Laurie, an' when Laurie's around, she's the one to catch your eye. Maybe I've been a chump."

Jerd nodded, but he really didn't think about Vanderveer's words. He was thinking of Namacho and the Apaches. They had made half a dozen passes at the house. They might try another, but sooner or later they would vary their attack. They would drop from their ponies and charge the windows. Some might get inside and, in an attack such as that, some of the defenders would go down. That was inevitable.

He took another look around the room. Seth Dawson was dead and probably, in one of the bedrooms, his widow was weeping over him. Maybe everyone here would die, but if not, and if they held the house, it could be done only at the expense of more tragedy. A few were single men but most of those here were family groups. Before the day was over, there would be more widows like Rita Dawson.

Another thought crossed his mind. He looked sharply at Bern Vanderveer. "Did Rogell put you here deliberately? You supposed to be watching me?"

"Just happened," Vanderveer answered, but he didn't meet Jerd's eyes.

"Think I'm with the Apaches?"

"Don't want to."

"But you're not sure."

"Didn't say that. But could be you don't like us too much here in Eden canyon. Could be you want to hit back."

"And maybe I have a reason."

Vanderveer squirmed uneasily. His answer was rather revealing. "I didn't have anything to do with the stage holdup. I didn't even go to the trial."

"But you know I wasn't guilty."

"Wasn't up to me to say one way or the other. Hell with it anyhow. That's all in the past."

"The money was never found," Jerd said. "They arrested the wrong man. I wouldn't say it was all in the past."

He heard the Indians coming again in another charge and he raised his head, listening. He thought he could detect a new pitch in the screaming, the shrill yelling whipped to a higher edge. He spoke half under his breath. "It's really beginning now. The beginning—or maybe the end."

Crouching, his rifle waiting, he watched the window.

Sam Rogell was forty-nine and, at least in his own opinion, he was in the prime of life. He had come to the Territory five years before, driving his own herd of cattle, aided by a hard-bitten crew, some of whom still worked for him. When he got here he had settled near Wickenburg and in a short period of time he made his influence felt. He was cattle wealthy, could drive a tough bargain, and in his dealings with others he was unencumbered by a conscience.

He had left a wife in Texas. Rogell let it be rumored that, as soon as possible, she would join him but he knew quite well she never would. Then later, when he needed some public sympathy, he let it be known that she had died tragically in an Indian massacre. Actually, she had divorced him.

Shortly after reaching the Territory, on a stagecoach trip he stopped at the Eden canyon station. The area interested him. He later made a trip there by himself, fell in love with the place, and decided that some day it would be his. At that time the barrens, embracing Eden canyon, were a part of the Indian reservation.

Rogell exerted every bit of influence he had toward changing the boundaries of the reservation and finally this was done. When the order came through, however, he was in Texas arranging another cattle drive. That delayed him for four months, then rumors of Indian trouble made him cautious. If he had moved to the canyon immediately, he and his men might have claimed most of the land. But they didn't, and one day he awoke to the fact that four settlers had claimed homesteads in the area.

In the next few months, Rogell bought out two of the settlers, took their land, and in the names of his men, claimed most of the lower canyon. But the prize spot of all, the place he had chiefly wanted for himself, had been claimed by a man who would not budge, who wouldn't sell out and who couldn't be frightened. That man's name had been Jerd Galway.

Eventually, and rather effectively, Galway had been removed. Or at least, he should have been removed. His arrest, conviction, and the long prison term looming ahead, made it impossible that he should continue to hold his land in Eden canyon. Normally, since Galway couldn't prove up on his patent, the land would be returned to the public domain and Rogell could grab it. And of course, that was what would happen. The fact that Galway had escaped really wasn't important. If something else didn't happen, the sheriff would get him.

Without much question, Rogell had been shocked when he ran into Jerd Galway this morning. And it was an upsetting thing to have to face an Indian attack. But while he could worry about the present, it was a habit of his constantly to look ahead. Everyone here might die, might be killed by the Indians. He was aware of that. But they might not die. They might be able to fight off the Indians, and if they did, and if Galway lived, his conviction would still stand.

As Rogell hurried toward the bedroom, he reviewed what he and Galway had just said. If he had to be honest with himself, he had to admit there wasn't much chance Galway had inspired the Indian attack. He himself could have done such a thing. It was a trick he might have appreciated. But Galway wasn't a clever man. He didn't have any imagination. He was a fool. Undoubtedly he had learned of Namacho's plans, and had rushed here to warn the settlers in the canyon, even if he knew it would result in his recapture. A fool thing to do. But he was a courageous man, too, and a courageous man could be dangerous. For that reason, any way Rogell could discredit him would be to Rogell's advantage.

When he reached the bedroom door he saw Laurie kneeling at the window's corner. She was in a fairly safe place, but still he rushed toward her and crouched at her side, pulling her lower. He spoke with a gruff and intentional concern. "Hey, I told you to keep down. I don't want you even scratched by an arrow."

Some of the Indians screamed past and a spear, hurled through the window, missed Rogell's shoulder by inches.

"That was a close one," Rogell said, and he used the occasion as an excuse to hug her.

She didn't twist away, which rather encouraged him. He had been having a difficult time with Laurie. He wasn't in love with her, as some people consider love, but she was an attractive woman, and, as his wife, she could be a credit to his position. In addition, through her father she would inherit some fine land in the canyon. Those were worthwhile considerations. In return, Laurie should have shown more interest in him. He was a damned important man in the Territory, well-to-do, and entirely masculine. She should have been an easy conquest but, for some reason or other, she had resisted him.

"Don't you worry about those Injuns," Rogell said. "I won't let 'em come near you."

"Is my father all right?" Laurie asked.

"Sure he is," Rogell said. "I told two of my men to keep an eye on him. Your mother, too."

He smiled and hugged her again, and he thought, *What do I care about her parents? If they both get killed, that would be fine.*

Over at the side, on the bed, Seth Dawson's body lay motionless. He was dead. His wife, Rita, was kneeling at the side of the bed, crying quietly. Rogell glanced at her, wondering abruptly what would happen to her and the land they had been working, far down the canyon.

It wasn't near his own holdings, but what of that? One of these days he meant to own the entire canyon.

His eyes had narrowed thoughtfully. Rita Dawson wasn't at all unattractive. She had been younger than Seth—was about thirty. And from what he had heard, she had a roving eye. Right now, of course, she was crying and seemed heartbroken but actually she and her husband had fought a great deal. In all probability she felt relieved that Seth was dead. He grinned wryly. Hell, lots of folks were like that. They seemed one way, but acted another. After a proper period of mourning, Rita would be a juicy plum, ready to drop into someone's arms. Maybe Bern Vanderveer's, who wasn't married, and who owed Rogell several obligations.

Laurie's high, shrill scream of warning saved his life. He jerked to look toward the window. An Apache was climbing into the room. He was carrying a short spear, had drawn it back and was ready to hurl it. Rogell twisted his rifle that way. He fired it, rolled to the side. The spear missed him by inches but the Indian, caught in the chest by a rifle bullet, rocked backwards and dropped from sight.

Another Indian took his place. This time, Rogell was ready for him. As he fired his rifle and the Indian fell away it occurred to him that what was happening was exactly what Galway had predicted, and if the Indians were trying to break in here, they would be hitting the other windows, all around the house. He heard shouting from the main room—he heard a woman screaming. He didn't know what was happening in the rest of the house.

A sudden fear struck at his heart. From the sounds he could hear, the Indians had broken in, and if that had happened all was lost. That is, all was lost unless he acted quickly. He could see no one at the window. The two who had tried to get in were dead. Maybe, for the moment, no one was outside. From here, it wasn't too far to the cornfield. If he could get there . . .

Rogell got to his feet. He moved to the window to look outside. He stared at the cornfield. Out of the corner of his eye he sensed a movement through the air, and instinctively, he ducked. But he hadn't been quick enough. Something struck against the side of his head and in a blinding burst of pain he lost consciousness.

As the Indians swept past the house, Midge was at the stove, pouring more coffee. She crouched close to the floor until the Indians were past. Inside, she felt terribly shaky. The experience she was going through was strange and unreal. The screaming Indians outside were a startling contrast to the grim silence of those inside the house. At two dozen places on the walls she could see feathered arrows which had sailed through the broken windows. Any one might have killed her—just as Seth Dawson had been killed. And at any moment, someone else might die.

Laurie, in one of the bedrooms, Mrs. Hale, Martha Carling, and several other women were handling rifles, just as the men. Even young Erb Ellsworth, hardly more than a boy, was fighting at the side of his father. Midge could ride with anyone, but she had never used a rifle. Tomorrow, if she lived that long, she would start practising. If she was to live in this frontier country, she would have to.

She had been carrying coffee to the men just to keep busy, and after the Indians swept past the house she stood up, lifted two filled cups, and turned toward the front of the room. But she took only a step and then stopped. At both front windows she saw figures climbing inside. Indians. Ugly men with horribly painted faces.

The men inside the house had been relatively silent, but suddenly they were shouting at each other, at the front, at the side, and at the rear. Shouting warnings, for at every window the Indians were trying to break in. Heavy blows were being rained on the doors.

In the next few minutes Midge caught a kaleidoscopic picture of what was happening all around the room, a confused, ever-changing scene. At first the men inside held the windows but then at the rear John Boulder fell backwards, a spear in his side and, too quickly to record it, the Apaches poured in. One, then another, and another, and another. More followed.

Two of the first to climb through the window were dropped but the third reached Mike Foss and they pitched to the floor in a rolling, grunting fight. Another rushed at George Odlum and one followed him, but switched his attention to Odlum's wife. Midge scarcely noticed that, however. One of the Indians was rushing straight at her—a short, thin man, his painted face twisted into a horrible grimace.

Midge hurled the coffee cups at him, and that seemed to stop him. But two coffee cups, she knew, couldn't have driven him back. Then, just at her side, she saw Jerd Galway, lowering his rifle. "Drop on the floor," he said harshly, and he seemed angry. "Don't make a target of yourself."

He rushed past her, and now he used his rifle as a club, and slashed with it from side to side. The two men he struck at went down and, from the side, John Boulder, in spite of the wound in his side, crawled toward one of the Indians, a knife in his hand. He used it again and again, stabbing at the stunned Indian. Jerd was clubbing the other.

Midge wiped a shaky hand across her face. Another Indian was climbing into the room. More would follow and, as that happened, the defenders inside would be overwhelmed. There was no hope for them. They were close to the end.

But, rather strangely, the confusion in the room grew no worse. At several of the windows, the fighting stopped. At the back of the room no more Indians tried to climb in. Mike Foss, who had been struggling with one of the Apaches, rolled the man's body aside and stood, wiping his knife on his trousers. John Boulder had collapsed, but the Indian he had reached was dead. And she was terribly afraid George Odlum's wife was dead. Her throat was bloody and she was stretched out on the floor, lying motionless.

"I think the Apaches have given up for the moment," Jerd said, raising his voice. "But some of you watch the windows. Hale, take a look in the bedrooms. And Vanderveer, you can help me pitch out the bodies of the Apaches we finished."

Midge took a ragged breath. She took another look around the room. She realized dully that the first attack was over. But from what she had heard she knew there would be another, and maybe another. And if the Indians kept driving at them, nothing could save them.

Jerd suddenly spoke to her, and his words were a command. "Midge, don't just stand there. There's work to be done. Shake up the stove. Put more water on to heat and find some bandages. Several have been hurt."

She managed to nod and she got busy, glad to have something to do. If a person kept busy it was hard to think—and right now, Midge didn't want to think, didn't want to look ahead.

Chapter V

THE INDIANS HAD disappeared. After the assault against the house had failed, Namacho must have called his men back to plan some new strategy. Dan Hale expressed a hope that the Indians wouldn't attack again, but Jerd was almost sure they would. He advised everyone not to go outside.

In view of what had happened, those inside the house possibly had done very well. But two of the men and one woman had been killed and several others had been wounded. Sam Rogell had a deep gash in his scalp, painful but not serious. Carling, Mrs. Hale, Joe Ingraham and young Erb Ellsworth had been scratched by arrows, some rather deeply. Mike Foss had a knife gash in his shoulder. The dead were John Boulder, a man Jerd didn't know named Sol Rhymer, and Mrs. Odlum. Earlier in the morning, Seth Dawson had been killed.

Laurie, Midge, Mrs. Ellsworth and Martha Carling cared for the wounded and, in spite of her bandaged arm, Mrs. Hale then supervised the cooking of breakfast. Jerd found a place for himself at the table. He hadn't eaten the day before and was terribly hungry, but most of those present didn't have much appetite. George Odlum, shocked at his wife's death, wanted only coffee. Rita Dawson tried to eat, but couldn't. Mrs. Boulder wouldn't come to the table. The others ate, but without much interest in their food.

"I know I'm making a pig of myself," Jerd said to

Midge, as she brought him another plate. "But I didn't
eat at all yesterday."

"I'm glad someone can eat," Midge said. "I'll bring
more coffee."

Jerd relaxed for a moment, resting his elbows on the
table. He glanced at Laurie, who was busy at the stove.
He hadn't talked to her since he arrived, although they
had had several chances. But Laurie had seemed anxious to avoid him. Twice since the Indian attack had
been broken he had caught her watching him. On each
occasion, however, when he noticed her she quickly
looked away.

Something bothered her. Possibly she didn't understand why he had escaped from the sheriff. Or maybe
the weight of her parents' opposition had influenced her.
What they needed was a chance to talk together but, with
all these people around and facing another Indian attack,
it might not be easy unless she helped.

Sam Rogell appeared from the second bedroom, where
he had been lying down. A white bandage circled his
head, making a startling contrast to his tanned skin and
the dark lower part of his face where he badly needed
a shave. This morning, shaken by what had happened, he
didn't seem nearly the commanding person he usually
was.

"Someone's got to go for help," he said suddenly.
"Who wants to volunteer?"

Jerd spoke quietly. "Take a look outside, Rogell."

"What do you mean?"

"No horses. The Indians collected all that were here.
Right now, they're probably raiding the places up and
down the canyon."

"Then someone'll have to walk."

"Through the sands of the barrens?" Jerd asked. "A
day and a half by horseback to Wickenburg—three days
by foot—and no water along the way."

"There's a stage station at Salt creek."

"Two days from here. Think you could make it?"

Rogell's voice had sharpened. "We can't just sit here.
We gotta get help."

Jerd shrugged. He turned back to the table and, as
Midge brought more coffee, he took a sip of it.

Hale, Ellsworth, Vanderveer and several more gathered around Rogell, and started discussing what to do. Jerd didn't try to listen to what they were saying. Instead, he thought about Namacho, and tried to figure out what he might attempt. Right now, of course, Namacho commanded all of the canyon, excepting the house here. He could loot and burn the ranches he found. He could drive off the horses. Such an accomplishment might be enough to satisfy him, but Jerd wasn't at all sure it would. Unless he was badly mistaken, Namacho would be back. It might happen before noon. Or maybe the next attack would be delayed until late in the afternoon. It was impossible to be sure what would happen.

Midge came toward him. Her question was direct. "What chance do we have, Mr. Galway?"

He shook his head. "I don't know, Midge."

"Could someone get away to get help?"

"I doubt it."

"Sam Rogell thinks someone could."

"Then you better talk to him."

She frowned thoughtfully. "No. I think Mr. Rogell knows about cattle and land and things like that. But I don't think he knows much about people. I suppose Indians are people."

"I believe they are," Jerd said.

"Did you really live with them?"

"I was captured by the Indians when I was too young to remember. I lived with them until I was fourteen."

"Mr. Hale calls them savages."

"At times they are—but so are we."

"But surely not in the same way."

"Three mornings ago, up in the Mesquite hills, I found a dead Indian. He had been shot in the back. His ears had been sliced off. A white man had done it."

"But every white man isn't like that."

"No. And every Indian isn't a savage. Years ago . . ."

He didn't get to finish. Rogell interrupted them. "Hey, Galway. We been talking about what to do. This is stage day."

Jerd looked that way, nodding. He recalled the stage schedule. Twice a week a stage run was made between Wickenburg and Eden canyon. The stage left Wickenburg the day before, stopped for a time at Salt creek, then drove on. If they got away from Salt creek by midnight, they could reach Eden canyon in the middle of the afternoon.

Rogell and the men around him were walking toward the table, and Rogell was speaking again. "Someone's got to get away, circle around and hit the road, meet the stage before it gets here."

Jerd was silent for a moment, but finally he shook his head. Everyone here was penned inside. If anyone tried to get away, he was dead.

"Don't shake your head at me," Rogell snapped. "It's got to be done. There may be women and children on the stage. We've got to stop them."

"How?" Jerd asked flatly.

"Damnit, I don't know. But it's got to be done."

"Maybe the stage line isn't running," Jerd said slowly. "Or if it is, maybe the driver will be warned by the smokes he'll probably see from the canyon."

"That's just a gamble."

"But it's more of a gamble to try to get away and warn the stage. With the Apaches all around us, how could anyone get away? Rogell, you're asking the impossible."

"Then we'll just let them die, huh? Is that it?"

Jerd showed a trace of anger. "Don't ask me, Rogell. If you want to warn the stage, go meet it yourself."

"I couldn't make it, and you know it," Rogell said. "There's only one man here who might be able to do the job—and that's you. You've lived with the Injuns. You've been a scout. If you could get away from the house, you'd know what to do—how to slip through the Injuns' lines. I'm asking you to try it."

"No thanks."

"You mean you're afraid."

"Sure, I'm afraid."

"A goddamned yellow-livered coward."

Jerd leaned forward and his eyes had sharpened. "At least, I'm not afraid of you."

"We'll see about that. We'll see."

Hale reached out to grasp Rogell's arm. "Drop it, Sam. We can't afford to fight among ourselves."

"But I'm thinking about those on the stage," Rogell said. "The women and the children."

"What women and children?" Jerd asked.

"Huh?"

"I asked—what women and children?" Jerd repeated. "We've all been at the station dozens of times when the stage came in. How often does it carry any women and children? Not once in a month."

Someone laughed. It was Lou Carling. He added a comment. "Seems like he's got you there, Sam. What women and children?"

"It could be there were women and children on the stage," Rogell said angrily.

"Maybe so," Carling said. "But let's not imagine things worse than they are. Sure I'd like to get a warning to the stage, but how anyone could get away from here in broad daylight, I just can't see."

The morning dragged. There was no more fighting. Through the windows Jerd could count the bodies of nine Apaches, slain in the attack. A few others, badly injured, might have crawled out of sight. But those remaining were a substantial number. At a guess, Namacho must have had more than a hundred warriors with him. They had disappeared temporarily. Some had gone away on raiding trips, up or down the canyon. Jerd could be sure of that by the smokes he could see in the sky, smoke from burning buildings. Perhaps all the Indians were gone, but he was skeptical about that. Some of the Apaches undoubtedly were watching the building here.

A mid-day meal was prepared. It was served in relays. And shortly after that, Sam Rogell made a general report to those present. Enough ammunition was on hand to last through several attacks—if everyone was careful, and if they made each shot count. They had enough food for a week. By tomorrow they would be short of water, but the well was nearby and during the night they might be able to carry in more.

All in all it was generally felt they were in fair shape to withstand a long siege—if that was what they faced.

Jerd Galway, however, didn't anticipate a long siege.

From what he knew of the Apaches, and particularly of
Namacho, he was fairly sure that the leader of the Indian band wouldn't want to be nailed down here in
Eden canyon. Namacho had meant to hit quickly. He had
meant to finish the job, then hit somewhere else. He
wanted to arouse the entire Apache nation through a
series of victories. He wouldn't want to spend several days
in a single engagement. To be brutally honest, the defenders were in a desperate position. Any time he wanted
to, Namacho could overwhelm them.

Why he hadn't pressed the attack this morning, Jerd
could only guess. Possibly, the Indians had called off the
fighting to make sure the rest of the canyon was in their
hands. That would have been a safe step. And it shouldn't
take too long. Maybe, by late afternoon, Namacho and his
warriors would be back.

Studying the problem they faced, Jerd took a look at
the defenders.

There were the Hales—Dan, his wife, and Laurie.
A man and two women.

There were the Ellsworths—Aaron, his wife and two
children. But during the attack young Erb Ellsworth,
about fourteen, had handled a rifle. He could rate the
Ellsworths as two men, a woman and a girl.

There were the Carlings—Lou, his wife and a baby.

There was Sam Rogell—but with him he had brought
Bern Vanderveer, Mike Foss, and Joe Ingraham. Four
men.

There was George Odlum, Rita Dawson, Alice Boulder and himself. Two men and two women.

To draw up a total, the defenders numbered ten
men, six women, a girl and a baby. Nineteen in all,
seventeen of whom could handle firearms. Seventeen
against a force of at least a hundred. The odds weren't
encouraging.

Turning to pace the room, Jerd noticed that for the
moment, Laurie was free and off by herself. He walked
that way, joined her and said, "Hello, Laurie. I've wanted
a chance to see you but you're always busy."

She motioned vaguely with her arm. "I know, Jerd.
But the way things have worked out—"

"How have you been?"

"One day's been just like another—up to this morning.
I—Jerd, do we have any chance at all?"

"Depends on what happens."

"Sam says we broke the back of the Indian attack. He
doesn't think they'll return."

"I hope he's right."

She looked at him thoughtfully. "You don't like Sam,
do you?"

"No."

"Why?"

"I blame him for what happened to me," Jerd said
honestly.

"But you're wrong, Jerd. You must be wrong. I know
that Sam is a little too aggressive, and men say he's hard.
But he has a background of violence. He had some
horrible experiences in the war. I know you think he
wanted your land here in the canyon, but that's just a
guess. I can't believe he would be so dishonest as to
ruin your life just for more land."

She seemed to mean it. Her voice was weighted with
feeling. Jerd didn't know who had talked to her, but
someone certainly had convinced her that Sam Rogell
was a fine man. He didn't know how to answer her. He
couldn't challenge what she had said for he couldn't
prove she was wrong.

She touched his arm lightly and she smiled. "I must
go now. Mother is signaling to me. We'll talk later—but
please, Jerd, don't be bitter about Sam. He's become a
good friend to all of us."

Jerd scowled as she walked away. He felt suddenly
impotent but through his bewilderment he could sense
a stirring anger. Sam was no fine, upstanding man. He
was too clever for that, too grasping, too harsh in every
attitude. One of these days, of course, Laurie would
see him as he was, but what Jerd could do, right now,
he didn't know.

The afternoon slid by without another Indian attack.
Jerd felt a deep relief. That meant the defenders had
another night, although how much that would help them
Jerd wasn't sure. A desperate plan had occurred to him,
but he was almost afraid to mention it.

As the sun went down most of the men gathered near the front windows. Rogell rubbed his hands together. He spoke in an authoritative voice. "The Injuns won't hit us again. It'll be dark in half an hour. The 'Paches are superstitious about fighting in the dark."

Jerd smiled wryly. The chief reason for avoiding a night attack was the darkness, when a man couldn't distinguish a friend from a foe.

"I'll tell you another thing," Rogell said. "We whipped the 'Paches for fair this morning. We hurled 'em back. They don't want no more of us. By morning, they'll be gone. More than likely, they're gone now."

Jerd walked forward. "No, the Apaches haven't gone. And they won't be gone by morning."

Rogell stiffened. "That's just talk. How come you know so much?"

"It's a matter of common sense," Jerd said. "Namacho hates us. He hates all white people. He broke off the attack this morning to raid the canyon but he hasn't left. We're the ones he's really after."

"I think he's had enough."

"Then you don't know Apaches."

"But I do," Carling said. "I spent six years as a trooper, and I agree with Galway. The Apaches haven't left. They'll hit us again in the morning."

Ellsworth shrugged. "I don't know who's right, but I don't want to be the first to go outside."

They went on talking, most agreeing the Apaches might still be in the canyon. Jerd edged around to the window. He looked across the yard and down the canyon road. The corn was high on either side. No one was in sight but that didn't prove a thing.

"Carling, did you ever do any scouting?" Jerd asked.

"Nope. Just soldiering," Carling said.

"Anyone else ever try scouting?"

"I did, for a time," Joe Ingraham said. "Don't know how good I am. What's on your mind?"

"As soon as it's dark, I'd like to take a look outside," Jerd said. "At least we could find if the Apaches are still in the canyon. Maybe we can locate their camp. If we creep close enough, maybe we can figure what to expect in the morning. Want to take a chance?"

Ingraham was tall, thin, stooped. He had a bony face, dark eyes, and thick, bushy hair. He might have been in his middle thirties. For a moment he hesitated, then shrugged. "Why not, Galway?"

"It ought to be dark enough soon," Jerd said. "Got any moccasins?"

"In my saddlebags—not here."

"I can loan you some," Hale said.

"Hope I can return them," Ingraham said wryly.

Jerd spoke again. "Don't wear your spurs, or your gun belt. Tuck your gun under the top of your trousers. Carry a knife where it'll be handy. Carry nothing in your pockets which might rattle. Wear no coat."

"Just be sure you come back," Rogell said, and there was an ugly suggestion in his voice.

"We'll be back," Jerd said. "I've got a special reason. It has something to do with a stage holdup several months ago and some missing money that was never found."

He stared straight at the man as he said that, but Rogell didn't blink an eye. He even seemed amused. "So you've come after the loot, huh?"

"Not exactly," Jerd said. "I'm here to point out the guilty man. I'll manage it, too, if the Indians don't get in the way."

He turned to the window, half angry at himself for what he had said. He couldn't do anything about Rogell as long as Namacho was outside, threatening another attack. Then, off in the cornfield to his left, he saw a movement which shouldn't have been there—a pressing of the stalks against the wind. He knew of only one thing which could have caused it. Below that spot, a figure was crouched close to the ground. One of the Indians.

Jerd forgot about Sam Rogell. He scanned the cornfield as far as he could see, but right now, the stalks were blowing the right way. At least, they were in no imminent danger of an attack.

Chapter VI

JERD STOOD AT the back bedroom window. It was getting quite dark outside. The early stars didn't give much light. Off to the side, Rogell was whispering to Joe Ingraham, but Jerd paid no attention to them. Several others were in the room and one of the men, it was Lou Carling, touched Jerd's arm and asked, "How long do you think you'll be gone?"

"Might take two hours," Jerd answered. "Or we might be longer. Hard to tell."

Ingraham left Rogell, joined them, and spoke gruffly. "How soon we be going?"

"Dark enough now," Jerd said.

"Which way?"

"Straight across the yard to the cornfield, work through it to the river, then look for the Indians' camp. Might be up river, might be down. We'll be damned careful leaving the house—belly down to the ground."

"Then let's get started."

Jerd swung through the window, stepped to the side and dropped to the ground. Ingraham followed. And for the next minute both hugged the earth.

The usual night wind had come up. It swept across the barrens and dipped into the canyon, singing through the trees and across the tops of the fields. It dropped lower to scour the clearing around Dan Hale's building. Through it, Jerd strained his ears to catch any sounds which didn't belong there and his head turned from side to side as he stared through the shadows.

From what he knew of the Indians, Jerd could assume that the Indians would have made a night camp, somewhere nearby. He doubted that Namacho had posted any guards over the house. Such a step wasn't necessary. Those penned inside Dan Hale's couldn't escape for the simple reason that there was no place to run. They were miles from any other settlement. They had no horses they could use.

Right now, in all probability, most of the Indians had

camped for the night. They would have built up a fire, and sitting around it, they undoubtedly were gorging themselves with some of the food they had collected at the ranches they looted. Surely at Rogell's, or at some of the other places, they would have found whiskey, to give an edge to the evening. Later, they would have a war dance which might last until midnight.

In spite of such festivities, however, some of the Indians would have crept close to the house, and would be watching. They would be off on lone hunts of their own for, if anyone ventured outside and some warrior could count a coup of his own, it would be a matter he could boast of. Jerd didn't doubt for a moment that several Apaches were prowling the darkness—and not very far away.

But he could see no one now. He could hear no one. Stretching out toward Ingraham, he touched his shoulder and motioned across the yard. Then, still hugging the earth, they worked themselves toward the cornfield.

Halfway there and off to the left, a shadowy figure loomed up in the darkness. Jerd reached out to squeeze Ingraham's shoulder, then he froze, and for a moment he thought the figure was moving toward them, or might have seen them. But he must have been wrong about that. The Indian came no closer. He apparently was staring at the house.

At his side Ingraham moved, raised his hand and, in the dim starlight, Jerd could see the man's gun. He reached out to push the gun down and, briefly, Ingraham resisted. But then he relaxed and a moment later the Indian swung away and, almost silently, vanished in the shadows toward the front of the house.

"I coulda got him," Ingraham muttered.

Jerd didn't answer but motioned ahead and they crept on, toward the cornfield.

When they got there they rested for a short time and could get up on their haunches. And, although he regretted it, Jerd felt he had to say something. He was blunt and direct. "We're not out after Indians. This is a scout. One bullet, and we might find a pack around us."

"Wasn't gonna shoot," Ingraham muttered. "Figured he was headed for us."

"If we do get jumped, use your knife," Jerd said.

He glanced at the man. Scouting an uncertain situation like this one, a man needed a partner, but now he half regretted that he wasn't alone. How dependable Ingraham was, he couldn't tell. On a scout, and in enemy territory, a man used his gun only as a last resort.

They crept through the cornfield and, from its far edge, moved as silently as they could through a thin stand of timberland to the river. The wind was blowing down canyon from the northeast and it seemed tinged with the smell of burning wood. That might be an indication that the Indians were camping up canyon, but Jerd couldn't be certain. The smell of burning wood could have come from one of the ranch houses which had been destroyed by the Indians.

Nevertheless, Jerd motioned up canyon, and he and Ingraham turned that way. They followed the stream for a mile and a half, then retraced their steps and went down canyon. This time they were more successful. In half a mile they came in sight of a campfire.

They approached it cautiously, hugging the ground as they drew nearer and, finally, from a screen of shrubbery scarcely a hundred yards from the fire, could study the camp. Some of the Indians were in a milling group, moving here and there. Others were seated, still eating. They were a noisy crowd, many boasting of the day's exploits. In the trees all around them they had tied their horses. A few weren't far from where Jerd and Ingraham were hiding.

"Must be a hundred of 'em," Ingraham said in a whisper. "You know their lingo. What are they yelling about?"

"They're boasting about what they've done today and what they expect to do tomorrow."

"You mean, they ain't pulling out."

"No."

"Which is Namacho?"

"He's there to the right of the fire—the man sitting all alone, under a blanket. After a time he'll call a council of the leaders, his sub-chiefs. Then they'll break it up and he'll wave a signal and they'll start a dance— a war-dance. It might keep on for hours."

"What if we could nail him?"

"It would save the Territory a lot of trouble, but I'm not sure it would save us."

"Wish I had my rifle."

"We'd better get back," Jerd said. "We're going to be needed in the morning."

He had seen and heard all he needed, but before he left the house he had guessed what he would find. The Indians hadn't left the canyon. With the first light of the morning, they would attack the house and this time, if the defenders threw them back, the Indians would attack again and again and again. In the end they would break into the house and probably they would manage it by sunup. They had the men to do it.

Jerd and Ingraham backed away, turned up river. They cut through the woods toward the cornfield. Since they had left the neighborhood of the Indian camp Ingraham had been complaining that they hadn't tried to get Namacho but Jerd paid little attention to him. From where they had been hiding an accurate shot would have been an impossibility.

"Still think I might have got him," Ingraham muttered. "If it hadn't been for you . . ."

He didn't get to finish. The three Apaches screened in the shadows hit them with no warning, two closing in on Ingraham, the third driving straight at Jerd. He saw the Apaches coming, saw the one sweeping at him, knife upraised, and he rolled to the side, grabbing at his own blade.

It was impossible to completely escape the slashing knife. A stabbing pain sliced down his upper arm. It felt like fire. But it was his left arm. His right was free and uninjured and, as the thrusting force of the Apache hurled him backwards, his right arm ripped upwards with his knife. He jerked it back, then stabbed again.

Ahead of where he had fallen, Ingraham was on the ground in a scrambling fight with the two Apaches. Jerd heard him scream, then scream again. Out of the corner of his eye he saw the two Apaches above Ingraham, stabbing their victim again and again. After the first moment, Ingraham hadn't had a chance. And after that second scream, he was silent and stopped struggling.

Jerd once more buried his knife in the chest of the
Apache who had carried him to the ground. He shoved
the body to the side, jerked to his feet and looked toward
Ingraham and the two other Indians. One was still slashing his knife at Ingraham but the other noticed Jerd and
swung toward him.

It was a temptation, but it was too late to help Ingraham. The man was dead. Jerd could do nothing for
him. Twisting away, Jerd raced for the cornfield. He
plunged into it and cut toward the house, not once
slowing down or looking back. He didn't have to. He
could hear the Indian chasing him.

Someone inside the house, posted at the front door,
heard him coming and, as he shouted his name, the door
opened. Jerd stumbled inside, closed it.

"Where's Ingraham?" someone demanded.

"He won't be coming," Jerd answered. "We ran into
some trouble."

"You mean you left him?" Rogell grated. "Left him to
the Injuns?"

"Couldn't be helped," Jerd answered.

He took a deep, shaky breath. He felt suddenly terribly
tired. His arm burned from the knife cut he had received.
And the news he carried wasn't good. In the dim light
from a turned-down lamp he looked at the people who
had gathered around him. Most of the men were scowling.

"We found the Indian camp," he said slowly. "It's
down the canyon a piece."

"Hell with that," Rogell interrupted. "I want to know
about Joe Ingraham."

"We were jumped by three Indians, just before we
got back."

"Yeah? Where?"

"Just beyond the cornfield. Didn't you hear the screaming?"

Rogell shook his head. "I didn't hear any screaming.
Anyone else hear anything?"

Several of the men made negative motions, then Rogell spoke again. "If it happened that way, someone
should have heard something. Maybe you better change
your story."

Jerd was abruptly angry. The implications in what

Rogell said were ugly. They amounted almost to a direct accusation. Jerd wanted to shout his answer. He wanted to challenge Rogell, but this wasn't the time for it. Everyone here faced a more important problem—the question of what to do about tomorrow.

"It's like this," Rogell was saying. "I've known Joe Ingraham for years. He was a damned good man. He could have handled any two Injuns in the country. Seems funny to me that Galway got back, but Ingraham didn't."

"That isn't the problem," Jerd said quietly. "I want everyone here to listen carefully. Ingraham and I found the Indian camp. We crept quite close to it. Close enough so that I could hear what was being said. The Indians aren't leaving the canyon. They'll still be here in the morning. They'll hit us again at dawn, and it won't be like it was before. They won't break off after a direct charge. They'll come again and again—too many to stop. We might last an hour. What we're facing is as bad as that."

The room was silent for a moment. Here and there, men looked at each other. Ellsworth put his arm around his wife, then, looking down at his daughter, he touched her hair. His face looked tortured. Martha Carling held her baby close. Her lips trembled and she started shaking.

"We held them off this morning," Hale muttered.

"Sure we did," Rogell said. "We'll hold 'em off again. Galway isn't scaring me any."

Carling shook his head. "Go ahead, if you want to. Sound as brave as you want to—but we all know the truth. We haven't got a chance."

"Just one chance," Jerd said.

He had the attention of everyone there. Even Sam Rogell had raised his head and looked startled.

"Before I talk about it," Jerd said, "I want to say something about what might happen in the morning. I doubt if the Indians will spend any time in riding circles around us. They'll hit the doors and windows and, if we hold them, they'll burn us out. It might take a little time to set the roof on fire, but once it starts, we'll be finished."

Carling leaned forward. "What's this one chance you mentioned?"

"I'm getting to that," Jerd said. "Since we can't defend the house, why stay here? In the next twenty minutes I'd like to see us make up food packages for everyone here. Then we'll leave, head up the canyon."

"But where up canyon? My place and Boulder's, the only ranches up canyon, were burned this morning. We saw the smoke in the sky."

"I mean to go really up canyon," Jerd said. "Beyond the narrows, up toward the headwaters of the river. In the rocky cliffs on either side there are a number of caves we could defend."

"But that's fifteen miles. We're on foot. And the women . . ."

"What about the women?" Martha Carling interrupted. "We can walk it."

Rogell shook his head. "We could never make it. The Injuns will be after us the minute we leave the house. If they catch us in the open . . ."

"I thought you told me the Apaches didn't attack at night," Jerd said dryly.

"Sure I've heard that, but what happened to Ingraham . . ."

"It's true enough, the Indians might attack us," Jerd admitted. "But there are several things in our favor. Without much question, Namacho expects us to stay right where we are. He's not anticipating that we might try to escape—there's no apparent place we can go. So he isn't watching us closely. Of course there are Indians outside and, before long, Namacho will learn that we've fled. But, by the time he hears that, we'll have a head start and the Indians will be in the middle of a war dance."

"They'll break it up," Hale said.

"Maybe so, but if we hurry we ought to be at the narrows before he catches us. We can stop him there for a time. We can fight a delaying action, all the way up the narrow canyon. Maybe we won't make it. Maybe the Apaches will close in and kill every one of us. But we're dead if we stay here. If we reach the caves we can hold out for a week. Namacho doesn't have a week. In four days, at least if the stage turned back, the Army will have been notified, and will ride this way."

To Jerd, that was a long speech. He smoothed back his hair, looked around the room. For the moment, no one had anything to say. Some of those facing him still looked startled, but that was understandable. What he was proposing was a radical step—a wild gamble. It might work, it might not.

"Think about it," he said. "But think quickly. If we leave for the caves, we ought to go as soon as possible —soon as we pack up the food. And if we go, we'll leave in a group, running, the men on the flanks and guarding the rear. We'll run until we're winded, then we'll walk. Then we'll run again. Before an hour passes your legs will cramp. Your feet will hurt. There'll be pains in your side but you'll have to keep on running—nearly all night. It's not going to be a picnic."

Alice spoke up. "What about—what about my husband's body? To leave him to the Indians . . ."

Jerd's lips tightened. "Nothing else we can do."

"If we could have a funeral . . ."

"No time for it, Alice."

"Then I don't want to leave."

"We'll all leave, or we'll all stay," Jerd said. "There are too few of us to split into two groups."

He looked bleakly around the room, particularly noting Rita Dawson and George Odlum, who were bereaved like Alice Boulder. What would they decide? What could he say to them to make their decision any easier? He could understand how they felt. It was true that Seth Dawson, John Boulder and Fern Odlum were dead, and couldn't be hurt any further by the Indians. But to leave their bodies here for mutilation was shocking.

Dan Hale cleared his throat. "Three of our close friends have been killed. If we could carry the bodies with us to a place where we could bury them . . ."

Jerd's answer was harsh. "No!"

"But it wouldn't take long."

"No. You just don't understand what we're facing. The Indians are mounted. We are on foot. I don't know how soon the Indians will follow us but if we ran all the way to the narrows we might not get there before the Indians overtake us. If we stopped to dig three graves, we'd never make it. I don't like to say such a thing, but I can't help it."

No one spoke. Alice Boulder twisted her hands together. She stared down at the floor.

"John Boulder is dead," Jerd said quietly. "Seth Dawson is dead. Fern Odlum is dead. But the rest of us are still living. We might escape. That's the choice you are making, Alice."

She took a deep breath. "Then we will go. But I think I hate you, Jerd Galway. I think I will always hate you."

Jerd shrugged. He made no answer. He hated himself, but he couldn't think about the dead. He couldn't think about the niceties of civilization. As a matter of survival, he had to think and act like an Apache.

He tried to put himself in Namacho's place. Undoubtedly, the Indians would soon learn of their flight and, unless he was mistaken, Namacho would think they had fled in terror and with no sound plan in mind. It was an Indian trick to seek a natural fortress. White people depended on artificial barriers. Because of that, Namacho might not rush after them, or might not catch up with them before they reached the narrows. If they were lucky, Namacho was in for a surprise.

Chapter VII

LAURIE STOOD AT the kitchen table working with several other women, wrapping up the food in bundles, and for the moment her mind was almost a blank. She couldn't think any more. She had lost contact with reality. The events of the day made everything seem out of joint. She had been shocked by the sudden appearance of Jerd Galway. Then, before she could recover, a dozen of her neighbors rode in. Hard on top of that the Indian attack had started and, in the bedroom right now, were the bodies of three of her friends who hadn't survived.

The remainder of the day, from sunup, had been a period of waiting, of uneasiness and tension, of uncertainty and fear. It wouldn't have been so bad if people had acted as she expected, but for some strange reason, nearly everyone here seemed to have changed. Aaron Ellsworth, usually a kind and gentle man, had turned into a tyrant. He snarled at his children, snapped at his wife and was ready to fight with anyone. The Carlings talked to no one but each other. Her father, ordinarily aggressive, seemed to have crawled into a shell. Sam Rogell, she no longer knew. He acted like a cornered animal, growling at everyone. And Jerd Galway frightened her. He seemed more calm than anyone else, but under the surface of his personality she could feel an explosive force, ready to burst.

Midge came toward her, touched her arm and said, "Laurie, someone should take care of Mr. Galway's arm. It's badly cut."

"You know where the bandages are," she answered. "You're not busy. This food ought to be bundled."

She looked to where Jerd was standing. He was holding his left arm. A tall, thin young man. He had a narrow face, high cheek bones and he was quite tanned—or brown. She bit her lips, frowning, wondering about the story her father had heard. Jerd had said he had been captured by the Indians, then had been repatriated following one of the treaties, but from what her father said, he was half Indian.

Midge's voice was low. "I think you ought to be the one to bandage his arm."

"Don't be foolish," Laurie said.

But she looked curiously at Midge as she said that. Her mind was working again, taking stock of her cousin. At this hour of the day and in view of all that had happened, Midge should have been reduced to a state of terror but she was bearing up very well. In fact, there wasn't any woman here who was doing any better. If Midge was frightened, she hid it. Her hands had been steady as she helped with the supper dishes and part of the afternoon she had held the baby for Martha Carling. Laurie's father had said jokingly, several weeks before, that Midge wouldn't be around very long, that some man would grab her and marry her but, at least in Eden canyon, that didn't seem much of a possibility.

"All right, I'll take care of his arm," Midge was saying. "But if you want to change your mind, let me know."

They were at the far side of the table and momentarily alone. Laurie spoke lightly. "Don't fall in love with him."

Midge smiled. "Why not?"

"He's going back to prison."

"Didn't you tell me he was innocent?"

"Yes, I did. And I think I was right, but the way the trial went . . ."

"If he was innocent then, he's innocent now."

Laurie bit her lips. "This is a practical world. Maybe Jerd can prove he didn't have anything to do with the stage holdup. But if he can't—and anyhow, there's something else you should know."

"What?"

"I'll tell you later. You're not really serious about Jerd Galway, are you?"

Midge shook her head. "Certainly not. I scarcely know him. But I wondered about you?"

"We were good friends," Laurie said slowly, and she was careful about the words she chose. "We might have been married if things had worked out. But they didn't. Then I heard—you had better take care of Jerd's arm while we still have time. He thinks we should leave as soon as the food is packaged."

"Then I'll get busy," Midge said.

Laurie tied up another bundle of food, then another. Her mother and Jane Ellsworth came back to the table to help and a moment later Sam Rogell walked toward her.

"You're a brave girl, Laurie," he said smiling. "What I regret more than anything else about the Indian attack is the fact that you're caught here. If there was any way to get you away . . ."

That remark, Laurie decided, was a typical Sam Rogell speech. He had fallen back into an attitude she could understand. Suave, courtly, genteel. She had heard he was hard, aggressive, a sharp trader, not a man to dodge violence but, at least until today she hadn't seen those sides of his character. In weighing him as a person she had been inclined to feel that in this frontier country some of those harsh points were unavoidable.

In her own mind she had half decided that some day she would marry him.

He came closer. "Are you nearly ready?"

"Yes, nearly ready," she nodded.

"Are you wearing comfortable shoes?"

"Very."

He scowled slightly. "It won't be easy—running through the night. But we won't let Galway push us too hard. He's getting under my skin, anyhow."

"If we have to run we'll have to run," Laurie said.

Rogell shook his head. "I'm not so sure of that. In fact, there's lots of things I'm not sure of about Galway. How come he got back, but Joe Ingraham didn't?"

"That was just the way things worked out."

"Maybe not. And maybe it wasn't an Injun that killed Joe Ingraham. Maybe the Injuns are gone and this whole trip through the night is just a scheme to trap us."

Laurie caught her breath. "Oh, no, Sam. You can't think he is as bad as that."

"He's half Injun. He's never admitted it, but I know it's true. He's a half brother to Namacho. I tell you, he's a man to watch."

"But to plot against his own people . . ."

"Which are his people?"

Laurie shook her head. She was upset because Jerd was here. She wished he hadn't come. Actually she was afraid of him, but she still couldn't believe what Rogell had said. He had gone too far in his accusations.

"Just don't get too near him," Rogell said. "But don't worry. I'll look after you."

He patted her shoulder, then turned away.

Laurie kept busy, but she was thinking about Jerd. When he had been arrested she had instinctively flown to his defense. That had been a natural thing to do. At that time, and in spite of what her father had said about Jerd, she had been resisting her father's antagonism. Throughout Jerd's trial she had maintained the same attitude of loyalty, even though secretly she had grown afraid she was wrong. Finally, after his conviction, she had had to admit she had been foolish.

The brief talk she had with him today hadn't changed her mind, particularly when he had tried to blame Sam

Rogell for his trouble. It was ridiculous to think that a man of Rogell's standing would stoop to banditry. And if Jerd had to go to prison and couldn't prove up on his land, it wasn't an incriminating thing if Rogell stepped in and took it.

Laurie's frown had deepened. Off and on, all day, she had been aware of Jerd's eyes, watching her and, without much trouble, she could imagine what was in his mind. He expected her to feel just as she had during the trial. He wanted to pick up the old relationship, at the same point. But people changed. It was impossible to turn back the clock. *I ought to tell him,* she told herself. *I ought to explain—but maybe I won't have to. Maybe the Indians* . . .

She couldn't complete the thought. Suddenly she was shaking. Her stomach started churning. She leaned against the table, glad it was there.

Midge dipped the cloth into warm water. She bathed Jerd's arm, then quickly started bandaging it. The cut in his arm was deep and she was afraid the bleeding would never stop.

"That's fine," Jerd said, nodding.

"It must hurt terribly," Midge said.

He grinned at her. "I can feel it. Now find a cord and tie my arm to my body so I can't move it. Unless we do that, it'll keep on bleeding."

She looked at him soberly. "What if you need the arm?"

"I carry a knife. If I need the arm, I'll free it."

"How soon are we leaving?"

"As soon as the food has been tied up."

She didn't look at him this time. "I've been thinking of Alice Boulder, Rita Dawson and Mr. Odlum. Isn't there any way—?"

His interruption was harsh. "No. There's nothing we can do for them. Think about something else."

"It wouldn't take long to bury the dead."

"It doesn't take long to die, either."

"If we leave the bodies here, what will the Indians do?"

"I told you not to think about it."

"You think I'm soft, don't you?"

He suddenly seemed tired, and he said, "Midge, I don't know. I don't like what I'm doing. I liked Seth Dawson, John Boulder. I've had coffee many times at Fern Odlum's house. I wish we could bury them, but we can't. We've got to think about the others."

"If we get to the narrows, will we get away?"

"I don't know."

Midge stepped away. "I'll get the cord to tie your arm to your body."

She went to look for one, half regretting some of the things she had said to Jerd Galway. It was the Christian thing to bury the dead and if it could be done they had that responsibility. But in a war, probably, some of the rules had to go by the board and undoubtedly this was a war. If Jerd was right in what he said she shouldn't have made his job any harder.

She found a cord, walked back to where Jerd was sitting and then tied his arm to his body. As she did, she noticed he was looking at her curiously. Then finally he spoke. "You're a strange one, Midge. Where are you from?"

"Ohio."

"Then you're new to the west?"

"But not to farming."

"You don't seem frightened."

She shook her head. "But I am."

"You're damned quiet about it."

Her lips twitched. "A person can be brave without blustering. Or he can be afraid without shaking. Would it be more convincing if I let you see my knees, knocking together?"

He nearly laughed. "Don't show me. It wouldn't be modest."

"I'm not always modest," Midge said.

She turned away and, as she crossed the room, her cheeks started burning. She wondered what had made her say such a thing. It had been a bold statement and really not true. The words had just blundered to her tongue and she had let them out without thinking. That in itself was a good indication of how she felt. Normally, she never would have said such a thing.

Rita Dawson had left the front bedroom where the

bodies of the dead were lying. She took a look around the big room, wiping her hand across her face. A rather attractive young woman, with very dark eyes, and dark hair. She had a nice figure, too. Off to the side, two of the men were watching her—Sam Rogell and Bern Vanderveer. As Midge passed them, walking toward Rita, she heard Rogell's voice saying, "Go ahead. This is a chance you shouldn't miss. Damnit, you know what to do."

"Hell with it," Vanderveer said. "We ain't got away from the Injuns, by a long shot. This is no time . . ."

That fragmentary conversation ran in and out of Midge's mind, and with no significance. She moved on to where Rita was standing and she said, "Rita, anything I can do for you?"

"What's to be done?" Rita answered. "Seth's dead. We'll all be dead by morning."

"Mr. Galway thinks we might escape."

"Who cares about that?" Rita said. "What difference does it make if . . ."

She didn't finish the sentence. Her eyes changed. They widened, then, quickly, they narrowed thoughtfully. She was staring over Midge's shoulder.

It was Bern Vanderveer. He came toward them, scowling, then he spoke in a mumble. "We're gonna leave in a minute. Maybe I ought to look after you."

"Why, that would be very nice," Rita said, and there was something almost coquettish in her attitude.

"You just stick close to me," Vanderveer said.

He took her arm, steered her away and Midge, watching them, knew she probably was being catty but couldn't help wondering how Rita had been able to forget her husband so quickly.

George Odlum and Alice Boulder left the front bedroom together, Alice terribly pale, hanging on to Odlum's arm. She seemed scarcely able to stand.

If we have to run, how can she do it? Midge asked herself. *Or how can Martha Carling run, with a baby in her arms? Or what about my aunt Ruth, whose legs were always partly crippled by rheumatism?* What Jerd Galway was asking was too much. It would be better to make their stand right here in the house.

Even as she decided that however, she heard Jerd's commanding order. "All right. We're ready to go. Everyone, take your firearms and a bundle of food. Gather at the back door. When I open it, out we go. And I want everyone running."

He gave more instructions, but Midge no longer was listening. Suddenly, overwhelmingly, she was frightened and terribly alone. She lived with the Hales, but she really didn't belong to them. She didn't belong to anyone. It struck her that if she disappeared, right now, no one would miss her, no one would notice. And that was a terrible thing to realize. It robbed your life of any purpose. It reduced you to nothing.

Jerd, talking to the others, individually or in groups, abruptly called her name. "Midge—Midge, come over here."

She walked toward him, but it was like walking through a dream. For a moment she was dizzy, then she steadied herself.

"I want you to stay with Martha Carling," Jerd was saying. "Take turns with her, carrying the baby. Think you can do that?"

"Yes, I can do that," she answered.

"Then, get your food bundle." He raised his voice. "Here we go. Hale, pull open the door. Lead the way. Cut to the road. Run two hundred steps, then walk a hundred, then start running again."

Someone opened the door. They started out. Midge turned to the table, took one of the few remaining bundles and then hurried to join Martha Carling. "I'll take your bundle, too," she offered. "Then we can switch when I carry the baby."

"I'm afraid to go out there," Martha said under her breath.

"So am I," Midge agreed. "But we can't stay here."

They were suddenly at the door and then outside and then they were running through the darkness of the night, following those just ahead. Midge was breathless before they started. She glanced from side to side, her muscles tensed against a sudden scream, the signal of an Indian attack. But there wasn't any screaming.

Someone passed them. It was Jerd, but in the darkness

he probably didn't recognize them. "You're doing fine," he called. "But don't slow down. Keep running."

To Midge, it seemed like a long time before the people in front of them slowed down to a walk. And then, before they could catch their breath, they had to run again. By now Midge had adjusted her eyes to the night. There wasn't much light from the sky but, from the bordering trees, she knew she was on the road up the canyon which went past the Carlings', and then the Boulders'. She had been that far on several occasions—and that was as far as the road went. Somewhere beyond, the walls of the canyon closed in.

Without thinking much about it, Midge had supposed the canyon ended not far past the Boulders'. But apparently it didn't. It ran much farther into the barrens, through a place called the narrows. She had no idea what it would be like, either at the narrows or above.

"I'll take the baby, next time we slow down," she said to Martha.

"I can manage," Martha answered.

But she was breathing heavily and once she tripped and nearly fell.

Midge started watching for Jerd. Twice he had passed them. Next time, she would stop him. They had to slow down. They couldn't possibly keep up this pace. It was impossible. She was young and in good condition but her legs were hurting, her feet were sore, her heart was beating too fast and her throat was raw from heavy breathing.

Suddenly they had a moment's relief. Ahead of them the people slowed and she and Martha stopped, Martha dropping to the ground.

Someone raced past them. It was Jerd. An instant later she heard his voice, harsh and angry. "Why have you stopped? Get on your feet and keep moving."

"We got to rest for a minute, Galway," someone answered, and Midge recognized her uncle's voice. "Ruth's legs gave out. There's a limit to what folks can do."

"But there isn't," Jerd whipped. "Ruth, get on your feet. We've got to keep moving."

Ruth Hale's voice was low. "I need—just a minute, Jerd. If you'll be patient . . ."

"I can't be patient," Jerd said, and his voice hadn't eased a bit. "We can't defend ourselves out in the open. First place we can make a stand is at the narrows, and that's miles from here. We can't lose a minute. Get on your feet."

"But I can't, Jerd."

He nearly shouted, "Get on your feet!"

Dan Hale broke in. "Damnit, Galway, you can't talk to my wife that way."

"I can and I will. Because I have to," Jerd answered. "I know you can't see anything out there in the darkness, but we've got a couple Indians on each side of us, and more following us. How closely Namacho is trailing us, I don't know. I'm afraid to think about him. If we stop we're dead."

"Then we'll drop out," Hale said stiffly.

"No, you won't," Jerd yelled. "Hale, get your wife on her feet. If you don't, I'll do it myself. We're going on. Now!"

Midge was shaking all over. Her hands were clenched. If Jerd had been near her, she would have hit him. Maybe he was right, and they had to hurry on, but there were physical limits beyond which a person couldn't go. Ruth Hale was half crippled by rheumatism. It was amazing she had gone this far.

Jerd's voice was a harsh order. "Ruth, get on your feet!"

Surprisingly, she did, and when she spoke she sounded almost apologetic. "I'm sorry I've acted this way, Jerd. Some way or other, I'll keep going."

"Good for you, Ruth," Jerd nodded. "All right, everyone. Start moving."

Hale's voice was low, heavy. "By God, you're pushing us too hard. Someday you'll pay for this."

If Jerd heard him, he didn't answer. He turned away, disappeared in the shadows.

Midge turned to the woman next to her. "I'll take the baby. I can handle the food packages, too."

"No. I'll take the food," Martha said. "But if you could take the baby for a time . . ."

"She doesn't weigh a thing," Midge said. "Start running. We're getting behind."

How far they had gone she didn't know. How far
they had to go she couldn't guess. Holding the baby in
both arms she hurried after the others.

Chapter VIII

BEFORE LEAVING THE house Jerd had picked up three
short spears. They had been hurled through the windows
by the Apaches. They were sharp-headed, the shafts
painted and tasseled. Once, years ago, Jerd had been
able to handle a short spear, rather effectively. Since
then he might have lost his skill but, at close quarters,
a spear was a good weapon. It could be launched quicker
than an arrow, and it was silent. Jerd wasn't sure he
would need them but they weren't heavy to carry.

He had tied his food bundle around his waist, carried
his rifle slung over his shoulder. His left arm was useless
but in his right hand he carried the three spears.

As they fled from the house, Jerd, by suggestion, re-
organized the group. He had two men in front of the
Hales, Mike Foss and Aaron Ellsworth. He had two men
in the rear, Lou Carling and Sam Rogell. Since he needed
Carling in the rear, he had put Midge with Carling's
wife. He had asked Laurie to stay with Jane Ellsworth
and the two Ellsworth children. Bern Vanderveer seemed
to have attached himself to Rita Dawson and, since she
was suffering from the death of her husband, Jerd didn't
want her left alone. For that reason, he left Rita and
Bern Vanderveer together. Similarly, Alice Boulder and
George Odlum seemed to be taking care of each other.
Hale had stayed with his wife, and Jerd hadn't objected
to that. He knew about Ruth's rheumatism. He knew
she would need help and encouragement.

In a way, Jerd had covered both flanks of their line of
march. Of course, he hadn't done a good job. No man
could. But he had made several trips into the shadows
on either side. They had left the house without trouble.
They were several miles up the road and no one had
attacked them. But he knew their flight had been noticed
and he knew that several of the Apaches were keeping

pace with them as they headed up canyon. That meant, undoubtedly, that someone had carried word of their flight to Namacho.

What to expect, however, he couldn't guess. Namacho might be satisfied to trail them through the night, expecting to close in at dawn. Or he might circle them and stop them before they could reach the narrows. Surely, if Namacho guessed they were heading for the narrows, he would block the way. That was the reason they had to keep running. They had to hurry, no matter what the cost.

The company fleeing the house had stopped briefly because of Ruth Hale. But they were moving on again, pounding up the canyon road. Jerd swung away. He stepped into the shadows to the left and started running. When he was well ahead of the others he angled into the bordering trees, then hunched down close to the ground in a screen of shrubbery.

The Indians trailing them undoubtedly were excited. Numbering only a few, and out tonight on a lone hunt, they wouldn't attack the group they were following, but should there be any stragglers they would die quickly. In that hope, the Indians kept close, watching a chance to strike.

Jerd, crouching in the darkness, heard the marchers pass along the road. And a shadowy figure slid through the trees. The first Indian was trailed by another. Then another. They made scarcely any sound as they went by. Jerd made little sound either but, as the third Indian passed him, he stood up, drew back one of the spears and then hurled it with all his force. He was close to the Indian. He couldn't have missed. The Indian tripped, spilled to the ground. A thin, startled cry broke from his throat, but it wasn't loud and it didn't continue.

Jerd waited where he was for a moment, half sure one of the other Indians would have heard the cry, and would turn back. But nothing like that happened. Jerd left the screening shrubbery. He stopped briefly at the side of the Indian he had dropped, made sure the man was dead, then took his place, trailing the two Indians somewhere ahead.

In half a mile he caught up with the second Indian, drew closer, and then used his second spear. Again, he didn't miss, but this time, the Indian screamed as he went down. The scream was high, shrill, and it could have carried a long distance. It came again, and this time, without any question, Jerd knew he would be in trouble if he stayed where he was. The Indian ahead would turn back. Those on the other flank of the road would swing this way. He could play a cat-and-mouse game with them, but that would pin him down here, and that was something he couldn't afford. He had to stay with the column. He had to keep them moving.

Jerd slanted away through the trees, aiming at the road. He came to it, raced forward, and caught up with the column sooner than he expected, for they had stopped again.

"What's wrong this time?" Jerd shouted before he reached them. "We're supposed to be heading for the narrows."

Rogell pointed into the darkness. "All that yelling— We thought . . ."

Jerd motioned with his arm. "Get moving. Aaron— Mike Foss—lead the way. And suppose we do a little running."

"But if we're gonna be attacked . . ."

Jerd swung toward Rogell. "If we are attacked, we'll be massacred. Our only chance is to reach the narrows."

"But that yelling . . ."

"One Indian. He ran into a spear. Get moving."

Ellsworth waved up the road. "Here we go. A hundred steps running, fifty walking. Keep up with us, folks."

Jerd trotted along with the others. He spoke to Jane Ellsworth and Laurie, young Erb Ellsworth and his sister. The youngsters were doing all right, and neither Jane nor Laurie had any complaints. Ahead of them George Odlum was running with Alice Boulder, holding her arm, urging her to keep going. Bern Vanderveer was keeping pace with Rita Dawson. Beyond them, Midge was carrying the baby, Martha at her side. Dan Hale and Ruth didn't look at Jerd when he joined them briefly. And neither spoke. From her breathing and from the way she limped, to Ruth this trip must be a torture.

They slowed to a walk, picked up to a trot, then slowed down again. Jerd pulled up with Aaron Ellsworth and Mike Foss. He motioned ahead. "How much road?"

"Ten or twelve miles, but I thought we'd turn off sooner, cut toward the river. If we stay to the road it'll take us at least two miles out of the way."

"Then save those two miles. What'll it be like along the river?"

"Cattle path along the river, halfway to the narrows. Above that, we'll have a rough trip. That's wild country. We won't do much running after we get there."

"Then we'll do it now."

Ellsworth shook his head. "Galway, we can't. Ruth's on her last legs, and there's others in the same fix. I'm tough as the next man, but my feet are killing me."

"So are mine. So what? You never know what you can do until you try it."

The man sounded angry. "Never thought it before, but right now, I can't help it. You're not human. You're cruel as the savages we're fighting."

"Not quite, Aaron."

"Are you, Galway?"

"What?"

"Half Indian?"

Jerd had heard that story before, but it had been pretty well killed. Now and then, of course, it cropped up again, and was used against him. As nearly as Jerd knew, and from such records as he had found, his father had been an Irishman from Pennsylvania. His mother had been a German immigrant. But since he had been raised with the Apaches and had acquired some of their characteristics, it was easy to hint that he was a half-breed.

"No, I'm not half Indian," he said slowly. "I'm as white as you, Aaron, if that's anything to boast about."

"Then prove it by the way you act. Don't drive us so hard."

"I can't help it. We're taking a long chance. If it was daylight, we wouldn't get a mile. As it stands now, I don't know what Namacho will do. If he thought we were heading for the narrows, he'd stop us. We've got to get there first."

"What if we do get there first?"

"It's a defensible position."

Ellsworth shook his head. "I don't know, Galway. We're trading the open spaces for a house we might have defended. Maybe we been tricked."

Jerd stared bleakly into the darkness. He was suddenly tired of argument, tired of whipping these people on. Maybe right now, to Aaron Ellsworth and to some of the others, the house they had left might be remembered as a sanctuary. But in the morning it would have been a death trap. Without losing a warrior, Namacho could have burned them out. Or in a direct charge, the Apaches could have overwhelmed them with their superior numbers. After some sane thinking, Ellsworth would agree, but with his feet hurting and unsure of the future, he was acting normally. He was reaching back to familiar things.

Off to the side, Jerd heard the sound of an owl. The call was answered from the opposite trees. But it wasn't owls who had made the sounds. Indians still flanked the column.

"We're coming to Boulder's cornfield," Ellsworth said. " 'Bout time to cut across toward the river."

"Turn any time you're ready," Jerd answered.

"If we could rest for a minute . . ."

"We can't. Keep the column moving."

Mike Foss spoke for the first time. "You're no goddamned boss. You can't tell us what to do."

"Someone has to."

"Then we'll call a vote."

"Call it after we get to the narrows," Jerd answered. "Those owl calls you're hearing aren't owls. They're Apaches, and they're all around us. This is no time to stop."

Jerd dropped back to run at the side of the Hales. He spoke to the woman, trying to encourage her. "You're doing fine, Ruth. We'll make it."

This time she answered. She sounded doubtful. "Jerd, if I can't go on . . ."

"We're half to the narrows. You'll make it."

Hale sounded angry. "Never should have left the house."

Jerd looked over toward him. "I'm counting on this,"

he said slowly. "The Indians are after us, but I don't believe Namacho has figured out what we're doing. Maybe he thinks we're looking for a place to hide, somewhere in the trees. I doubt if it's occurred to him that we might head for the narrows, or to the caves up the river. If I'm right about that, Namacho won't push us too hard. He'll trail us and laugh at our frantic race. He'll expect to close in on us, soon as it gets light. But before then, we'll be at the narrows. And if we get to the narrows we can make a stand."

"How?" Hale asked bluntly. "The Injuns will still outnumber us, five to one."

"But we won't be penned in a house they can set afire. We'll have cover to fight from. And, as I remember it, the river is deep at the narrows, and on each side there's a tangle of shrubbery. With six men we could hold off an army."

"The Injuns can climb out of the canyon and cut us off behind."

"But not for several hours. Not until we can get a good start for the caves."

Hale shook his head doubtfully. "Sounds all right, but I ain't sure it'll work. Maybe you're Injun enough to fight half in the open. Most of us ain't."

He sounded bitter. He sounded like Ellsworth. Jerd was suddenly convinced that if he put it up to a vote, right now, nearly everyone here would regret they had left the house. But they were tired of running. It seemed like a long way to the narrows and then up to the caves. And, at any moment, the Indians might attack. It was easy to understand their feelings.

They reached the cornfield and turned through it. Jerd stepped to the side, stopped briefly, and looked around. Under the pale light of the stars he could mark the progress of the column and then, off to his right and off to the left, he could sense in the movement of the corn the flanking Indians. More than he had expected. Possibly a dozen. But at least the main body of the Apaches hadn't caught up with them.

Jerd stooped over to rub his legs. His feet were killing him. Early this morning he had stumbled up to Hale's, nearly crippled from the miles he had run across the

barrens and into the canyon. He thought then that for
a week he wouldn't be able to walk. But here he was
again, on another run. He could almost agree with Ruth
that they might not reach the narrows.

Jerd sighed, then tried to forget about his legs and
hurried after the column. He caught up with the rear
guard as they left the cornfield and turned under the
trees in the direction of the river.

Rogell whipped up his holster gun and swung toward
him as Jerd came in sight. Above the gun, Rogell's
scowling face stared at him. And for a moment, the
gun wasn't lowered.

"Thought you was an Injun," Rogell said. "Nearly shot
you. Maybe it's too bad I didn't."

Jerd shrugged. He made no other answer.

"Where you been?" Rogell continued.

"Checking on the Indians," Jerd said, and he frowned.
He didn't want more trouble with Rogell, at least right
now.

"You mean you was making a report," Rogell said. "I
got half a mind to drop you, 'fore it's too late."

"If you really thought I was working with the Indians,
you'd have killed me before this," Jerd said. "You don't
even run a good bluff. Suppose I try one. What did you
do with the money you took from the holdup?"

"You're the one who did that."

Jerd smiled, shook his head. "Met a man in jail. He
was one of the passengers on the stage the night it was
held up. He admitted he had been paid to identify me."

"That's a damned lie."

"Nope. I'll prove it. And I can prove another thing.
One of your men, Mike Foss, said he'd seen me cutting
toward my place from the Wickenburg road, the night
of the holdup. When I get the chance I'm going to work
on Foss. Make him tell the truth."

"He told the truth. If you monkey with Foss . . ."

"That's only the beginning," Jerd said. "Let's turn back
to my first question. What happened to the money?
Ten thousand dollars. Been spending any money lately?"

Rogell was still holding his gun. He was short of
breath from running, flushed, and his nerves must have
been on edge. He suddenly swung his gun toward Jerd

and his words came in a shout. "By God, we'll settle this right now. We'll . . ."

Jerd didn't have to answer. Lou Carling, running beside them, reached out and knocked down Rogell's arm. He spoke harshly. "Save your bullets for the Apaches, Sam. No time now for personal quarrels."

"But I won't take a thing like this," Rogell snapped.

Carling swung between the two men. He glanced at Jerd and said, "You, too. Drop it until we finish with the Apaches."

The column was slowing to a walk. Just ahead of them, Laurie looked back. She must have heard most of what they had said, but it was impossible to see the expression on her face. Jerd waved to her, then he spoke to Carling. "All right, Lou. I'll ease up on Rogell, but tell him to drop his talk that I'm working with the Indians."

He moved on past the others to the head of the column. Off to his left, through the trees, he could see the starlight on the shimmering water of the river. They had reached the bordering cattle trail.

"From here, we're gonna have to go single file, most of the way," Ellsworth said. "And perty soon, the trail peters out. It won't be easy after that."

"Pick out the best way you can," Jerd answered. "And keep moving."

"We been hearing lots of Indian calls. Think they'll hit us?"

"Hope not. If we keep moving, they might just trail along. How far to the narrows?"

"A long two miles."

"The last part of it, we've got to race."

"What we been doing already?" Ellsworth asked angrily. "Quit nagging me."

"Just keep moving," Jerd said. "Keep moving as though the devil was breathing on your tail."

He dropped back to tell the others what was ahead. Ruth was limping terribly. Hale had been helping her, holding her arm, but at times, now, he wouldn't be able to.

"Only two miles, Ruth," Jerd said.

She didn't answer, didn't look up.

"It'll be single file, part of the way," Jerd said. "But you can make it, Ruth."

"If we can't, we'll drop out," Hale said harshly.

Jerd shook his head. "You'll keep moving. Keep your place in the column."

He was glaring as he swung back toward Martha Carling and Midge, and Midge surprised him. She spoke quickly, "Don't snap at us. We heard you. Part of the way we have to go single file."

"I wasn't going to snap at you," Jerd said.

She lowered her voice, "Ruth is doing wonderfully well. If you were more kind . . ."

He felt a sudden irritation. Then he noticed that she had given the baby back to Martha but instead was lugging four food bundles, hers, Martha's, Dan Hale's and Ruth's. A good twenty-five-pound load. Midge was doing more than her share.

"I'm sorry, Midge," he said slowly. "Some people you have to whip, some you have to beg. Maybe I've been too rough with Ruth."

"If you want to catch flies, use honey."

That gave him a chance to grin. "Who wants to catch flies?"

"But you know what I mean."

He nodded, then dropped back to talk to Odlum and Alice Boulder. She was staggering nearly as badly as Ruth. She was a thin, intense woman. Her husband's death seemed to have been a shattering blow.

"Don't worry about us," Odlum said thickly. "We'll keep up with the others."

"It'll be single file pretty soon."

"Makes no difference."

Odlum didn't look up. His answers were spiritless. But then, just as with Alice, he had suffered a deep personal loss.

Rita Dawson was cut from a different mold. Vanderveer was helping her, but Jerd suspected she didn't need such assistance. She didn't seem exhausted.

"If we have to go single file, I'll be right behind you," Vanderveer told her.

"If it wasn't for you, I'd just die," Rita said.

The words were so extravagant, even Vanderveer

seemed uneasy. He scowled at Jerd and spoke gruffly. "Don't worry about us. We're doing all right."

Behind Vanderveer and Rita, Jane Ellsworth asked about her husband.

"He's a good leader," Jerd said. "You're a brave one, too. And the kids."

"I'm no kid," Erb Ellsworth said.

"They're really not," Laurie said. "Kathie's grown up, even though she's only eight. She hasn't complained once."

"And you, Laurie?" Jerd asked.

She shook her head, switching the subject from herself. "I heard what you and Sam were saying. You are each unfair to the other."

"My fault, probably," Jerd said. "Looks like here's where we have to go single file. Keep close to the one in front of you."

He stepped behind Laurie, then looked around. Rogell was following. Carling behind him. Jerd looked ahead again. He thought of the thin line along the trail, and he knew that if Namacho hit them now, they wouldn't last more than a minute. He didn't like this at all, but what he could do about it, he didn't know.

Along here the shrubbery pressed in on both sides, crowding the trail. Thorny branches scraped at him, snagged at his jacket. The tangle got worse but at least, if it was hard on them, it was also a hindrance to the Indians.

Less than six months before, Jerd had been up here with John Boulder, on a fishing trip. They had tried a deep pool, just below the narrows, but to get there had been an adventure. This entire end of the canyon was a tangle of greenery, shrubs, thickets, and trees. The few animal trails wandered indiscriminately in every direction except straight. There was no direct route to the river or to the narrows.

As they pressed along the twisting trail they were following, Jerd wondered what Namacho was thinking, if he knew where they were. Probably he did, and probably he thought they were trapped in this tangled wilderness. There was a way out, of course. The narrows. But to Namacho, that shouldn't seem like an escape.

What was beyond it? Just a long, narrow canyon, twisting into the rolling sands of the barrens, surely no sanctuary.

They were moving too slowly. Jerd raised his voice, "Pass along the word—we've got to move faster. Faster!"

Off to his right an owl call sounded, terribly close. Another Indian answered—then another, and another. Jerd could feel his muscles tightening. They had just passed another branching trail. They would come to others. At half a dozen places the Apaches could cut their column into sections.

He shouted again. "Faster! Faster! We've got to get to the narrows. It can't be far off."

Under the trees and in the darkness he couldn't see the closing walls of the canyon. Maybe they still had a mile to go, but he hoped he was wrong about that. Right now was the time when they should be hurrying. They were almost within striking distance of their first objective.

"Faster," he shouted. "Faster! We're almost there."

He repeated that cry several times and, in spite of the narrowness of the trail, in spite of the scraping branches which tore at them and in spite of the weariness of everyone there, they did move faster. Ahead of them, Laurie tripped. She fell to her knees but she was getting up even as he reached her and she indicated she wasn't hurt. Others might have stumbled and fallen to the ground but if they did they got up again.

The trail turned toward the river, then away. It had become an up and down trail, its progress marked by low ridges. Off to his right and now behind him, Jerd could hear the owl calls of the Apaches. Some of them had fallen back. An encouraging sign.

Then he heard another—Ellsworth's voice raised in a triumphant cry. "We've made it. The narrows. They're dead ahead."

There were answering shouts from some in the column and for a moment Jerd could relax. But only for a moment. It was worthwhile to make the narrows. It probably was worth a celebration, but he knew quite well that this wasn't a victory. The hardest part of their campaign was still ahead.

Chapter IX

CENTURIES AGO A fingering range of the Sierra Robles had stretched out to the west. Once it might have been a high, proud ridge, towering above the ground. In time, however, the encroaching sands had stormed its sides and nearly smothered it. Today only traces of it showed above the rolling swells of the barrens.

The river it had fathered was more enduring. From some deep reservoir a clear, cold water rose to the surface. It struck out to the southwest, digging a channel to mark its course. For the first ten miles Lost river was hemmed in, in a narrow, rocky canyon; but finally, as though resenting such confinement, the waters of the river carved a wider bowl, a broad and fertile valley. In ten more miles Lost river spent itself and sank out of sight, but the richness of what men called Eden canyon probably was worth it.

Jerd had made his first trip to the canyon as an Apache youth, accompanied by Namacho and three others. Their journey here had been an adventure. The Indians had never lived here. They called it the Canyon of the Buzzards and there was a taboo against going there. Completely different from the surrounding area, the Indians were suspicious of it.

Tonight, as Jerd climbed through the narrows, he was reminded of his earlier journey into the canyon. In those days, long ago, he and Namacho had climbed in the other direction, daring each other and their companions to walk the full length of the river. It had taken considerable courage. They had felt excited. And after it was over, both he and Namacho had boasted that some day they would return.

Well, they had returned as they promised, but hardly in the way they expected.

The narrows were giant granite blocks, nearly a hundred feet high. They stood possibly forty yards apart. Half of that distance was water, the deep channel of the river. It cut nearer the north wall. To the south there was more land, a sloping tangle of shrubbery, possibly twenty yards wide. Up the canyon, at most places, it was wider than right here. But not much wider. And the walls of the canyon, in general, were quite sheer.

Beyond the narrows and along the animal trail, the column stopped. Nearly everyone dropped to the ground, grateful for a chance to rest. But all of them couldn't rest—or if they did, they would have to do it in a guarding position.

Jerd turned to Sam Rogell and Lou Carling. "Watch our back trail," he ordered. "The Indians aren't far behind us. One will be crawling this way any minute. Nail him when you see him."

"What about the river?" Carling suggested.

"I'll get some men down there, right away."

He asked Ellsworth and Mike Foss to creep down to the river. Undoubtedly some of the Apaches would brave the water. But to breast the current would be a noisy venture and the men guarding the bank should hear them.

After these emergency measures had been established, Jerd took time for a cigarette, as he looked ahead. The Indians would try the narrows, but after a few shots, would drop back. If they made any determined effort to move ahead, it undoubtedly would be put off until dawn. But Namacho wasn't limited to the narrows. His warriors were mounted. Some could climb out of the canyon and turn up this way. By eight in the morning, maybe earlier, some of the Apaches would be on the rim of the canyon above them.

He didn't have to worry about those on the rim too much. Arrows or spears hurled from the rim would be caught in the air currents and accurate shooting was impossible. Those with rifles had a better chance but the rifle was such a new weapon to the Apaches that most hadn't become experts.

As a greater danger Jerd had to worry about a band of Apaches who might streak up the rim of the canyon to a place where they could climb down. There were a number of such places. Jerd didn't know exactly where they were. He doubted if Namacho knew. But Namacho could find them, and if he did so quickly, the settlers could be cut off before they reached the possible security of the caves.

Jerd walked to where the Hales were sprawled on the ground. He knelt down near them and said, "Ruth, how are the legs?"

She shook her head. "Don't ask, Jerd. If I had to walk another step, it would kill me."

"No, it wouldn't, Ruth. You're going to surprise yourself. By the time the sun comes up, you'll be half up the canyon toward the caves."

Hale motioned angrily with his arm. "That's enough, Galway. We're staying right here. We can hold the narrows."

"How about the canyon behind you?"

"No Injuns up there."

"But they can get there, Hale."

"Then we'll throw up a barrier right here."

Jerd shook his head slowly. "We could try it, but the caves would be better. A few of us will stay here for several hours. We'll hold the narrows, long enough for most of you to reach the caves, then we'll join you. We'll . . ."

"No, by God. We're staying here. Sam! Aaron! George! The rest of you. Come here a minute."

"Sam's busy. So is Aaron. I don't see why . . ."

"Then I'll tell you why. You been acting like a general. And by God, you're no general. We'll take no more of your orders."

"Someone has to give orders."

"Not you."

"Then take over yourself, Hale. But start most of the folks up the canyon. Nothing else we can do."

Sam Rogell joined them, towering above them. "Got Bern to take my place on the trail," he said gruffly. "What's all the argument about?"

"Galway's handing out orders," Hale said. "I've had enough."

"Me, too," Rogell said.

They were interrupted by a rifle shot back up the trail. It was followed by another. Jerd whipped to his feet. He hurried to where Carling and Bern Vanderveer were lying. Carling pointed into the darkness.

"He came out of nowhere," he whispered. "One minute, wasn't anyone there. Then all at once, I saw him. One of the Apaches. Dropped him, but he crawled back. Had to shoot him again."

"They'll try again," Jerd said. "Keep awake, Lou."

"Think they'll rush us?"

Jerd shook his head thoughtfully. "I doubt it, Lou. The underbrush is thick—only this animal trail they can use. If they come single file, we can drop them, one by one. A few shots like that ought to be damned discouraging."

"Then what?"

"Then they'll climb out of the canyon and try to get behind us. That's why we've got to reach the caves."

He turned away, stopped at the side of Jane Ellsworth, Laurie, and Rita Dawson, who had joined them. Kathie was half in her mother's arms. Erb was sitting up, his rifle across his knees.

"You get maybe five more minutes to rest," Jerd told them. "After that I want you to start up the canyon. We'll send two men with you."

"Only five minutes?" Jane said wearily. "I could sleep a week."

"That comes later," Jerd grinned. "How are the kids?"

"I'm proud of them," Jane said. "Don't worry about the children."

"You, Laurie?" Jerd said.

She nodded but didn't speak. It was too dark to see her eyes, but he could feel her watching him. He thought again, *I've got to find a time to talk to her*, but when that time would come he didn't know.

"Stay where you are," he told them. "I'll let you know when to move on."

It occurred to him then that he had an argument on his hands which hadn't been settled. But to hell with that. The argument could be settled in only one way. It might be several days before any help would reach them. Long, hard days. If they didn't have to worry about Indians reaching the upper canyon, they could have defended the narrows. But, caught in the middle and with more Indians up on the rim, their position here would be-

come impossible. They had no choice but to drive on
toward the caves.

Alice Boulder was lying face down on the trail, as
motionless as though she was asleep. George Odlum sat
at her side, his shoulders sagging. A short, thick-bodied
man. Middle-aged, usually rather quiet, unassertive. He
and Fern had had two children—a daughter who had
just married and moved to Prescott and a son boarding
in Wickenburg and going to school.

Jerd stopped. He said, "George, how do you feel?"

The man looked up bleakly. "I don't know. I suppose
I'm tired, but all I can think of is Fern."

"You've looked after Alice."

"The blind helping the blind."

"Someone had to do what you did. Is she sleeping?"

"I doubt it. But I don't think she wants to talk to you.
I don't want to talk to you, myself. Why in hell couldn't
we have taken the time to bury our dead? We're still
civilized people."

His voice had tightened angrily. His eyes were hard and
unforgiving.

"I did what I thought we had to," Jerd answered.
"We've got to think about the living. We're dead tired but
in five minutes most of us have got to start up the canyon."

"Alice can't make it."

"She'll have to."

"People can take only so much."

"But how much is that, George? How much is your
life worth? You haven't even started to use the strength
you've got. No one has. Quit acting like a child."

Odlum jerked to his feet. "By God, no one can talk
to me like that."

"Good. Get mad," Jerd said. "That's the kind of
spirit we need."

He moved on. Ahead of George Odlum and Alice
Boulder, Martha sat on the ground, nursing her baby.
Midge was beside her and as she looked up, Jerd smiled.
He said provokingly, "I noticed you carrying the baby,
but there are some things you can't do for her."

"If she was mine I could," Midge said instantly. "Na-
ture provides for such things."

"You've got me there," Jerd admitted. "How do you feel? Able to take another walk?"

"If I have to, but I'd rather not."

"How about you, Martha?"

"Don't worry about me. Just tell my husband to be careful."

Midge leaned toward him. "How about Ruth? Jerd, if there was any way . . ."

He made a negative motion. "No, Ruth will have to go on with the others. Some will stay here, to hold the narrows. When we leave, we'll be running. And we'll have to keep it up. But if the rest of you leave now you can take it easier up the canyon, rest now and then."

"At least, that'll help."

He could talk to her as though he had known her for years, but, in a rather annoying way, he couldn't reach Laurie at all, and that was entirely wrong. Surely, no one here should have been able to understand him better than Laurie. Of course, he hadn't had much time with her, but to be honest, that didn't explain how he felt.

Scowling, Jerd looked ahead. Ruth was stretched out on the ground, resting, but both Dan Hale and Sam Rogell were facing him, waiting for him. And from their attitudes, he was going to run into opposition.

They didn't wait to hear what he had to say. Hale jumped at him instantly, and with a proposition. "Galway, we've been talking. We ought to have a leader. Thing to do is have everyone vote, then we'll . . ."

"No time for it," Jerd interrupted. "After we get to the caves and settle down for a siege you can vote until you're blue in the face. The thing to do right now is get most of the folks on their feet and started up the canyon."

"But that's just the point, Galway. Some of us ain't in shape to head up the canyon."

"Who isn't?"

"Ruth for one."

Jerd looked down at her. "Ruth, are you awake?"

The woman stirred. "I'm awake."

"Then listen," Jerd said. "And you, Hale and Rogell, listen. I'm not going over it again. For a time we can hold the narrows, but by dawn there'll be Apaches on the rim, shooting down at us. And maybe by ten o'clock in the morning several parties of Indians will have found a way to climb down into the upper canyon. That will leave us in a trap and with poor cover. If we want to live through the next few days the only way to do it is reach the caves. Ruth, it's maybe ten miles to the caves—a hard, long walk. Can you make it?"

She turned on her side, looked up. "I can try."

"There's your answer, Hale," Jerd said flatly.

"But there's no such all-fired hurry," Hale said. "If we had an hour's rest . . ."

"No, Hale. Those ten miles are long and hard. We've got to start now. Every step we take is a step nearer the caves."

Sam Rogell leaned forward. "You make things worse then they are. Hale, I'm for meeting to choose a leader. And it won't be Galway."

"Then choose anyone," Jerd snapped. "But before you do, one of the three of us is going to get the folks started on up the canyon. Hale, you can give the order. Or you can, Rogell. Or I will."

Rogell shook his head. "No, by God."

Jerd swung around. He raised his voice. "All you folks I spoke to. On your feet. Time to start up the canyon."

Rogell reached forward to grab Jerd's arm. "Now, wait a minute, Galway."

This was a critical moment and Jerd knew it. He twisted free, jerked around and spoke under his breath. "Keep your hands to yourself, Rogell. If you've got anything to say at all, help me get these people moving."

Rogell showed his quick, driving temper. "Like hell! Before we decide anything, I want to hear from everyone else. If I've got to use my gun . . ."

He reached for it but, as he drew, Jerd's slashing arm cut across his wrist and knocked the gun from his hand. As it fell, Jerd struck at the man again, smashing him squarely in the face. The blow was hard enough to stagger Rogell, knock him off balance. He tripped, fell on his back and lay there, seemingly dazed.

Dan Hale looked shocked. He raised his hands toward Jerd in futile protest. He cried, "No, Galway. We can't . . ."

"Rogell isn't hurt," Jerd said. "Help Ruth to her feet.
And, Hale, I want you to lead the folks up the canyon.
You and George Odlum. You've been to the caves, haven't
you?"

"Sure, but . . ."

"Walk fifteen minutes, rest five and follow that pattern
all the way. I want you halfway to the caves, by sunup.
And every step of the way I want you to remember this.
*By morning, some of the Indians will be climbing down
into the canyon. If you move fast enough, you won't
meet them. If you move too slowly, you'll never make it
to the caves.*"

"What about the men left here?"

"There are enough of us to fight our way up the canyon," Jerd said.

He hoped he was right about that, but he wasn't at
all sure. If only a few of the Indians climbed down in
the canyon, they could handle them. If there were too
many, they would be trapped.

Ruth Hale was on her feet. She got up without any
help—a gaunt woman, her face pale and deeply lined.
She brushed back her hair, took a deep breath and said,
"Dan, shouldn't we get started?"

Behind her, Martha was carrying the food bundles and
Midge was holding the baby. As they passed Jerd,
Martha said, "Look after my husband, please. He's too
—too reckless. I want him to see his daughter grow up."

"I'll do all I can," Jerd promised.

"Don't forget to catch up with us," Midge said.

He nodded, then looked at Alice Boulder and George
Odlum, who were next in line. Alice didn't look at him.
She was staring straight ahead. Odlum was scowling.

"George, I want you folks to drop out and form the
rear guard," Jerd said. "Keep the line close together."

"You and your damned orders," Odlum muttered.
"One of these days . . ."

He didn't finish the sentence but he reached out to stop
Alice, then they stood at the side while the others passed.
Jerd spoke to Jane Ellsworth, young Erb and his sister, to
Rita and finally Laurie. But it was a hurried meeting.

"Laurie," he said to her, "Rita is here to help Jane
with the children. When you have the chance it might

be a good plan to catch up with your mother. She could stand some help."

"I will," Laurie nodded. "But I'm not sure what I can do. Mother's always been terribly independent. She's stronger than she looks."

He touched her shoulder lightly. "Look after yourself, too."

"I'll manage," Laurie said.

She flinched away from his touch, or perhaps he was wrong about that. Perhaps she was just turning to move on after the others.

Alice and George Odlum fell in behind the column.

In a few steps the column was out of sight, heading up the canyon. Two men, seven women, two children, and a baby. An even dozen. If they hurried enough, they ought to reach the caves without any trouble and there they could defend themselves.

Left here at the narrows were Jerd, Sam Rogell, Bern Vandeveer, Mike Foss, Aaron Ellsworth and Lou Carling. Six men, all well armed, none seriously injured.

Jerd made a brief appraisal of the problem they now faced. He had two men watching the river, Ellsworth and Mike Foss. He had two men guarding the trail, Carling and Vanderveer. Probably for the moment, that was enough. The Indians might test the narrows again but they would delay any heavy attack until it was light. At that time he would double the number, locking the trail. Four men, carefully handling their guns, could do terrific damage to any Apaches who tried to rush the narrows.

But that was only one phase of the problem. Right now, undoubtedly, Namacho knew they were holding the narrows. And Namacho was a savvy Indian. He might attack at the narrows, but he also would send men to the rim of the canyon, to shoot down at the defenders. In addition to that, almost certainly, some of the Indians would be sent to climb down behind the narrows. That would take time, however. Before the Apaches could climb down into the upper canyon, they would have to find a trail. It was possible they would stumble on such a trail shortly after dawn. Or it could take longer.

Jerd hoped the Indians would find a trail into the

upper canyon, within a mile or so of the narrows. In that way those who were hurrying to the caves wouldn't run into a fight. But he couldn't be sure what would happen.

Rogell was sitting up. He looked to where his holster gun had fallen and to his rifle, standing against a tree. Neither was within reach. He spoke suddenly, angrily. "This is your chance, Galway. Maybe the only chance you'll have. When I get my hands on a gun I'm going to kill you."

"Why not call a truce until we finish with the Apaches?"

"No."

Jerd took a deep breath and then nodded. "All right. Get your gun. If we've got to settle things right now, we will. But we'd be a damned sight smarter if we waited."

Rogell's eyes narrowed. He seemed to think for a moment, then said, "A truce, huh? Until we finish the Apaches?"

"Why not?"

"I think you're with 'em. I think you've led us into a trap."

"Then get your gun, Rogell. This is a good place to die."

"You'd like that, wouldn't you?"

"No. I want you to live, just long enough to tell the truth about the holdup of the Wickenburg stage."

"Fat chance anything like that will happen. It's a matter of record who held up that stage—a man named Galway."

"But you and I know differently. So what do we do, Rogell? A truce, or crawl over there and get your gun? We can settle things right now."

Rogell's smile was crooked. "You're too damned anxious. We'll call a truce."

Jerd shrugged, then stood watching as Rogell got up his holster gun, then his rifle. He seemed suddenly confident, assured. That the Apaches were just beyond the narrows didn't seem to worry him.

"You'd better join Vanderveer and Carling, up the trail," Jerd suggested.

"What are you going to do?"

"Check with Aaron and Mike Foss, down on the river."

"I don't like to think about you, sneaking up behind me."

"I don't blame you. You're guilty as hell."

"And you're dead."

They stood facing each other. For a moment Jerd thought Rogell was going to grab his gun. But he didn't. Instead, after a momentary hesitation, Rogell swung away and headed up the trail to join Vanderveer and Carling.

Chapter X

OUT IN THE OPEN canyon Rogell had scarcely noticed the wind. It had been blowing, of course, but not hard. In the narrows, however, the wind was strong and it seemed to carry a chill. He turned up the collar of his coat, wished futilely that he had a bottle and then took a look at the sky. The moon was up and had been for several hours. It brightened the night and directly above the stars were out. The edge of the wind had made Rogell expect to see clouds and a storm building up. Perhaps that was happening but from the depths of the canyon he couldn't be sure.

Turning up the trail to join Lou Carling and Bern Vanderveer, he made his own analysis of the problem they faced. The Indians had been stopped at the narrows. Possibly for a long time they could hold the narrows. But if they tried it, if they stayed where they were and if the Indians got behind them, they would be trapped. Rogell didn't want to be trapped.

He stopped briefly to consider what he ought to do. Without much question Jerd Galway had done a smart thing in making the people race up the canyon. If they had stayed at Hale's, they would have been an easy prey to the Indians but if they made it to the caves, they could hold out for days. They had a sufficiency of food. Several of the caves housed springs where they could get water. And surely, in another week, the army would find them.

Unfortunately, however, they weren't at the caves. Part of them were on their way, working up the animal trail along the river, and by mid-morning should have found a defensible position. That was wonderful for them. But what about him and what about the others left here at the narrows? He shook his head, scowling. Maybe the narrows had to be held in order to give the women a chance to get up the canyon. And maybe it was a fine, sacrificial thing to throw away your life to protect someone else. But so far as he was concerned, he wanted no part of it.

Rogell moved on. In half a dozen more steps he came to the place where Carling and Vanderveer were guarding the trail. One was on the left, one on the right, both crouching low to the ground and under the protection of outcropping rocks and a tangle of shrubbery.

"You better get down," Carling warned. "Someone up there on the trail, not far ahead. Got a glimpse of him a minute ago an' I can tell you this. He ain't friendly."

Rogell hunkered down on the ground, near Carling. It hit him abruptly that Carling was enjoying this adventure. He probably was worried as hell about his wife and baby. He never would have admitted he wanted this to happen. But since it had, he had dived into it head-first. It fed some inner need in his body. Once, Rogell remembered, Carling had been a trooper. Then he got out, married and settled down to the hard work of a farmer. But maybe, as a trooper, he had loved the service, the fighting and the rowdiness of the barracks. A few men were like that. Reckless. Foolish. Not worth a damn. But such men could be used.

Rogell mentioned the women. "They're gone—headed up the canyon."

"Heard 'em leave," Carling nodded. "Glad they're gone. It's a long trip to the caves and some of the women ain't in good shape. Have to go slower. That's why we got to hold the Apaches here."

"But what about us?"

Carling looked around. "You scared, Sam?"

"Hell, no," Rogell answered. "Just been thinking. If

the Injuns get behind us, we'll be in a jam. 'Course, I'm
all alone. Don't make much difference what happens to
me. But you got a wife and a baby. What about them?"

"If they get to the caves, they'll be safe," Carling said.
But he was scowling, suddenly thinking of them, worried.

Rogell smiled. He decided if it came right down to
cases, Lou Carling would do considerable thinking about
his wife and baby. He would want to rejoin them. He
wouldn't want to be trapped.

Sitting back, Rogell took another look at the situation.
He had thought of slipping away alone, before it was
too late. But if he did and the others also escaped, he
would find himself branded as a coward. Better than
that was another plan now forming in his mind. A very
practical plan. He went over it slowly, nodding his head.

If it came to a test of strength between him and Jerd
Galway, he could claim the loyalty of Bern Vanderveer
and Mike Foss. Both worked for him, took his orders.
That left Lou Carling and Aaron Ellsworth who might
follow Galway—an equal division of power. But actually
it wasn't at all certain that Carling and Ellsworth would
turn against him. Each had a family to worry about.
Each man surely wanted to live. And neither had close
ties with Galway. It seemed to Rogell that if he handled
the situation cleverly, he could take Galway's place.

He didn't think he had to worry about Mike Foss. To
be honest, Foss was a brutal man, crude and violent,
a man whose guns and conscience could be bought—
and at a low price. Some day soon Rogell was going
to have to get rid of him but right now it was good
to know he was here. He would follow orders. Bern
Vanderveer, however, was a different kind of person.
He could be as brutal as Foss and he had done some
ugly things in the past. But sometimes he hated himself and he wasn't wholly predictable.

To make sure of him, Rogell crawled to the other side
of the trail, drew nearer Vanderveer, and then spoke.
"Things seem damned quiet. What are we worried about?"

"They're out there—in the darkness," Vanderveer
said. "I've heard 'em."

"They're not rushing the narrows."

"They can hear, too," Vanderveer said. "They know

we're waitin' for them. Soon as it gets light, we'll have our hands full."

"Then what if we stay here, and what if the Injuns get behind us?"

Vanderveer shook his head. "Hope they don't. Or at least, too many of 'em. If they do, we're finished."

"Then why don't we head up the canyon, before it's light?"

"Can't," Vanderveer said. "Got to give the women a chance to reach the caves. That's a long trip."

"Too bad," Rogell murmured. "You seemed to be getting some place with Rita Dawson. She's a fine-looking woman."

Vanderveer was suddenly frowning. He was silent for a moment, then he said, "Hell with it. Who knows what'll happen? Maybe we'll all make it up the canyon to the caves."

Rogell left things as they were. For a while, he wanted Vanderveer to think about himself and Rita. And he could give Carling a chance to think about Martha and the baby. Besides, it probably was smart to hold the narrows for a time. He took a look at his watch and was surprised at the hour. It was later than he had thought. In three more hours it would start getting light.

Settling down in the darkness, Rogell made his plans. He was in good physical condition. He still had a deep wound in his scalp, and he could feel it, but that had little effect on his legs. If he had to, he was sure he could run most of the way up the canyon to the caves. If they left, then, an hour before dawn, and left running —and if they were quiet about their departure they should get nearly an hour's start on the Indians. If they left that early, they shouldn't run into any Indians in the upper canyon. It should be mid-morning before the Indians could find a trail from the rim.

Rogell was startled by a sudden burst of rifle fire, down on the river. He heard three shots, then two more.

"Several Apaches, trying to breast the river," Vanderveer guessed. "Don't figure they made it, or we'd have heard more excitement."

Rogell started to speak. "What if . . ."

He was interrupted by the crash of Vanderveer's rifle. In the shadows up the trail he could sense a thrashing movement. Through it he could hear a crying, choking sound. Then, rather abruptly, everything was quiet.

"Got him," Vanderveer said. "But there's plenty more where he come from."

"Too many," Rogell said.

He meant it, and if the Indians got behind them, no one here would escape. But if they did leave an hour before dawn they would have a chance. The women, by then, should be nearly to the caves. He checked that in his own mind. It was only ten miles up the canyon to the caves. Anyone on foot should make three miles an hour, even if the trail was hard, and if the people walking it were tired. It was a long time since Rogell had had to walk anywhere, but still, the analysis he had just made seemed reasonable.

Jerd Galway came up the trail, silently as a shadow. Rogell didn't hear him coming, was startled to see him and, instinctively, swung up his rifle.

"It's just me," Jerd said, and he seemed amused. "Everything quiet?"

"Got another Apache," Vanderveer said.

"Mike Foss and Aaron got two," Galway said. "They were swimming up the river, hugging the far bank. Nearly missed them. Foss must have eyes like an eagle."

"He's a good man," Rogell said.

"I'll bring him up here, toward dawn," Jerd Galway said. "Or maybe earlier. One man can hold the river. Up here along the trail, we'll be busy."

"How long will we hold the narrows?"

"At least until eight. We want to give the women a chance to reach the caves. The minute we leave, the Indians will be after us. If we catch up with the women too soon, we'll be caught in the open, and that would be fatal."

Rogell didn't challenge him. Foss was going to be brought up the trail and that was good. He could wait for that. Then, with Foss and Vanderveer to back him, and maybe with the support of Lou Carling, he could take charge. And to hell with Jerd Galway. If he wanted to stay here and be a hero, let him.

It was a slow and torturous trail up the canyon. Slow to everyone and torturous to people like Ruth and Alice Boulder. But then, it was hard for every one of them—Dan, who had to lead the way, and George Odlum, who guarded the rear and kept driving them to hurry. Martha was limping, too. She had tripped and fallen, and had cut her knee.

Midge thought she had done very well, thus far. She wasn't hurt, and if she was tired, what of it? At least she was better off than most of the others. She could think clearly, too. She could appreciate the need for hurry and, in a quiet way, she had done all she could to keep the column moving. Again she was carrying Martha's baby, and two food bundles were tied around her waist.

Several of the people here amazed her. Ruth, in spite of her limping, and the gasps of pain which sometimes escaped her, stubbornly kept on her feet, and did no whining. And both George Odlum and Dan Hale nagged them to keep moving. Strangely enough, when Jerd was driving the column, both men had resented his orders. In a position of authority, however, they adopted Jerd's methods. Alice Boulder was having a hard time keeping up, and that was true of Laurie, which Midge couldn't understand. Laurie was short of breath. Several times she had stumbled awkwardly and once she hadn't wanted to get up. Young Erb Ellsworth pulled her to her feet. He was quite a boy.

They hadn't done any running since leaving the narrows, but that wasn't their fault. Maybe what they were following was a trail, but it was so overgrown they couldn't run. At times the underbrush was so tangled they could scarcely get by. Midge's jacket was so snagged it was ruined. Her face had been scratched several times. That had happened to everyone else, too.

Toward dawn, when they stopped again briefly to rest, Midge gave the baby to Martha, then edged up the trail to where Laurie was lying. She had stretched out on her side, her face buried in her arms. Just ahead of her, Ruth was lying on her back. In the first pale light of the morning she seemed asleep.

"It's been quite a trip," Midge said, dropping down

near Laurie. "But we're getting up the canyon, at least. We must be more than halfway to the caves. What are they like?"

"I don't know," Laurie said, and she sounded very tired. "We'll never get there. At least, I won't."

"Why not?" Midge asked. "To get there, all we have to do is keep putting one foot in front of the other. Before we realize it, we'll be there."

"But I'll never make it."

"I will," Midge said. "After the beating I've taken this far, the entire Apache world won't stop me."

Laurie shook her head. "You don't know what you're saying. We're trapped. We'll never see the men we left back at the narrows. In another hour, the canyon will be alive with Indians."

"Where will we put them?" Midge asked. "In the trees or on the tops of the bushes? From what I can see, this canyon is so narrow and so choked up with shrubbery, the Indians would have to go single file, just as we are doing."

"You don't know what they're like."

Midge smiled. "At least, they can't fly. A canyon wall is still a canyon wall. And a tangle of shrubbery is hard to get through."

Laurie looked up at her. "You're almost flippant."

"Not flippant. Practical. We're still alive. Somewhere ahead there are caves we can defend. We might not get there, but at least we can try."

"Jerd got us into this," Laurie said.

Midge frowned. "I don't know what you mean."

"He was arrested for holding up the Wickenburg stage. After he was caught, some of those in the canyon had to testify against him. That made him bitter. It made him want to get even. After he escaped, he fled into the barrens, turned back to the Indians. He's a half-breed. His mother was an Apache. You didn't know that, did you?"

"No, I didn't," Midge admitted. "I heard he had lived with the Apaches, but I thought he was captured when he was quite young."

"That's the story he tells, of course. But it isn't true."

Midge was still frowning. "Do you really think Jerd brought the Indians here?"

"I don't want to think such a thing, but Sam says . . ."

"Sam doesn't like him."

"That has nothing to do with the matter. Sam is . . ."

They were interrupted by Dan Hale. "Time to move on," he shouted. "On your feet everyone."

He was as gruff and insistent as Jerd had been when he had been urging them to hurry. Farther down the trail, George Odlum picked up the order and repeated it.

Midge struggled to her feet. She looked at Hale and asked, "Aren't we more than halfway?"

He peered at the gaunt, sheer walls of the canyon. "Almost halfway."

"Is the trail like this, all the way?"

"For several more miles it'll be like this. Then the walls widen a little. We come to some boulder fields. The caves are in the north wall of the canyon, across the boulder fields." He raised his voice. "Everyone up. Time to move on."

Midge dropped back to rejoin Martha Carling. "Want me to carry the baby?"

"I'll carry her this time," Martha said. "I wish Lou had stayed with us. If they don't catch up with us . . ."

"They will," Midge said.

She tried to believe that, and she tried not to think about the Indians.

Occasionally, they talked and this time, as they moved on, Midge asked about the stage holdup, and then asked, "Were people sure Jerd was guilty?"

"Everyone seemed to think so," Martha answered. "One of the passengers identified Jerd—and at least, he wasn't home that night. Mike Foss went to see him, but his house was dark."

"Doesn't Mike Foss work for Sam Rogell?"

"I don't know why that's important."

"Did they ever find the money?"

"No."

"What happened to Jerd's land?"

"I suppose the patent will be turned over to someone else."

"Sam Rogell?"

"No. According to the Homestead Act, a man can file on one hundred and sixty acres, and that's all."

"But couldn't Sam have one of his men file on another one hundred and sixty acres, then later, buy the patent? Don't things like that happen?"

"But what does that prove?"

"I don't know," Midge said.

The trail grew harder. They stopped talking. But Midge couldn't stop thinking. Perhaps Jerd had been guilty of the holdup. Perhaps he was half Indian. And perhaps he had brought the Apaches to Eden canyon. But the missing money was a valuable prize, and so was the land Jerd had lost. She looked up, then caught her breath. *On the rim of the canyon and against the grey sky of the morning, she could see the figure of an Indian!*

Chapter XI

AT THE EDGE of the river just inside the narrows, Jerd crouched at the side of Aaron Ellsworth. He looked up at the sky. It was still dark. But in the next half-hour it would change and the shadows would gradually thin. "I want you to stay here, Aaron, and guard the river," Jerd told him. "The Indians may not try it, but we can't be sure of that. I'm going to move Foss up the trail to help Lou Carling, Vanderveer and Rogell."

"You've given me the easy job," Ellsworth said. "There'll be more action on the trail."

"Don't worry," Jerd said. "Before the day's over, you'll see all the action you'll ever want."

He motioned to Foss, backed away, then turned up to the trail.

Foss stopped him before they reached the others. "How come you picked me to defend the trail?"

"You're a better man with a gun," Jerd said honestly. "Aaron's been a farmer. He can sight a rifle but you're ten times as fast. If the Apaches try to rush the narrows, we'll need you."

"Good chance I'll get killed, too."

"Same chance I'm taking. Would you like to know a

secret? If possible, Foss, I'm going to keep you alive,
just so you can admit you lied at my trial."

"Never do that."

"I think you will. If I have to, I'll beat the truth out
of you. But not until we've finished with the Apaches."

"That's one of the craziest things I ever heard."

"Suppose we move up the trail. Ought to find cover
while it's still dark."

They crept the last few yards. Then, near Vanderveer and
Rogell, they stopped. This land between the narrows was a
slanting shelf, running from the south cliff to a twenty-
foot drop at the edge of the river. It was covered by a
tangle of shrubbery, open only along the animal trail. If
the Indians wanted to gain the narrows, they had three
choices. They could go up the river. They could take the
trail. Or they could climb into the upper canyon, somewhere above. The current was too swift to make the river
practical. It would take time to reach the upper canyon.
That left them the trail—and it was the trail they might
rush.

Lou Carling was above the trail, and under cover.
Vanderveer and Rogell were below it, and that was the
approach Jerd and Mike Foss had taken.

"One of us will join Carling," Jerd said. "That will give
us two men above the trail, three below it. Aaron is
guarding the river."

"How long we gonna stay here?" Rogell asked.

He had asked that question before. Jerd answered him
again. "Several hours. At least until eight. We want to
give the women a chance to reach the caves."

"Only ten miles up to the caves," Rogell said. "Ought
to be there now."

Jerd slightly raised his voice. "Carling, you ever been
up the canyon?"

"Tried it once," Carling answered. "Didn't make it far.
Maybe there's an animal trail, but at places it's so overgrown it's nearly impassable."

"How long do you think it'll take the women to get
to the caves?"

"Maybe mid-morning. Maybe noon."

"There's your explanation, Rogell," Jerd said. "It's impossible that the women could have reached the caves. If

we left now, the Indians would be right behind us. If we caught up with the women before we reached the caves, we'd be left in the open."

Rogell's voice had sharpened. "And what if the Injuns climb down in the canyon, right where the women are? What if we ain't there to help them?"

"I think it's more likely that the Indians will climb down in the canyon, somewhere just above us. I think they'll turn this way, toward us."

"You think, you think, but you don't know!"

"That's right, Rogell."

"So we'll be trapped."

"We'll have a fight on our hands to reach the caves."

Rogell made an angry, sweeping motion with his arm. "No, by God. I don't intend to be trapped here in some fight while the women may need our help. Right now, and while we got a chance, I'm for heading up the canyon."

"The women haven't reached the caves," Jerd said. "We'll stay here."

"I vote the other way," Rogell said. "So does everyone else. Foss, put your gun on Galway."

Mike Foss shifted position. Perhaps he drew his gun, but it was too dark for Jerd to see clearly. Then the man spoke, and he sounded puzzled. "Put a gun on him? Why?"

"Damnit, who you working for?" Rogell snapped.

"Been working for you," Foss admitted. "But since the Injuns hit us, I been thinking about myself."

"You want to stay here and get trapped?"

"Nope. Can't say I want to get trapped. But it wouldn't help us much if we caught up with the women, afore they get to the caves."

"But we're dead if we stay here."

"Maybe so. Don't know. What do you think, Galway? If we stay here and hold the narrows several hours, think we might make it to the caves?"

"We can try it," Jerd said.

"How do you reckon our chances?"

Jerd shook his head. "You figure it. When we leave here, the Indians will be chasing us. On the way, we may run into some more. I'm counting on it. We might fight our way to the caves. We might not."

"You mean, the odds are all against us."

"That's right, Foss."

Rogell spoke again. "And that's why I'm for leaving now—while we can."

"Sure," Foss said. "We could leave now, but we'd catch up with the women and that would bog us down. Think I'll string with Galway. Not that I'm on his side. I'm thinking about myself."

"I'll remember that, Foss," Rogell said angrily. "How about you, Bern?"

"I'm restin' easy, right where I am," Vanderveer said. "Figure we ought to give the women a chance to reach the caves."

Jerd wished he could have seen Rogell's face. But he couldn't. It was too dark. He could imagine, however, the expression that was there—a mixture of anger and surprise, frustration and bafflement. His own men had turned against him. Not actually, of course, but at least they hadn't followed his lead.

"I'll slide across the trail, join Carling," Foss said. "But before I do, tell me this, Galway. How many Injuns we gonna run into up the canyon?"

"If I had to guess, I wouldn't say it was too many," Jerd answered. "Namacho will keep most of his men with him. He might send several parties up the rim, to cut behind us."

"But how many?"

"Maybe a dozen. Maybe more."

"A dozen, huh. That's not as bad as it might be."

"It takes only one arrow to drop a man," Jerd said caustically.

"You're a hell of a cheerful guy," Mike Foss said.

He scrambled across the trail and it was well that he hurried. An arrow, whistling through the air, couldn't have missed him by more than a few inches. Up the trail, hidden in the shadows, one of the Apaches had caught a glimpse of him.

"They're still out there," Vanderveer muttered. "Wish they'd show themselves."

"You'll see them when it gets light," Jerd said. "Give them another hour."

"If they don't come too fast, we can choke up the trail with their bodies."

"It won't be as easy as that," Jerd said.

Rogell had nothing to say. He had dropped lower, under the protection of a rock shelf. He seemed wholly at ease. Certainly he had dropped his argument that they should leave.

Jerd looked toward him. It occurred to him abruptly that if he looked away Rogell might crawl off and, when he had a chance, flee up the canyon alone. He might make it, too, and undoubtedly if he caught up with the women he would have a sound explanation. But damnit, if the Apaches made a strong attack on the narrows, he needed Rogell here. He had only five men to hold the trail.

Crawling closer to him, Jerd spoke under his breath. "Don't try it, Rogell. We need you here."

"Hell with you, Galway," Rogell snapped. "I'll do as I damned please."

"No, you'll help us hold the trail."

Rogell raised his head to make an answer, but apparently he changed his mind, and was silent. Then he dropped down again. Jerd rolled to his side to look up at the sky, wincing as he remembered his injured arm. From deep in the canyon he couldn't see much of the sky, but it didn't seem as dark as it had been. Morning wasn't far off.

The air swept above them but, dipping lower, made a constant rustle through the shrubbery. To those sounds was added the rush of the water churning through the narrows, slapping at the rocky banks. Those noises Jerd had learned to know. He listened to them without hearing them. His ears were tuned to any sounds which normally didn't fit that pattern. A crackling in the thickets or a new splash in the water he would have heard.

But for several hours now the Apaches had made no definite attempt to broach the narrows. A probing expedition up the river had been tried, and failed. Warriors scouting the trail had learned how far they could go with safety. More might have tried the trail but, at a guess, Namacho had cautioned them to await the morning.

He could afford to do that. The Apaches had a superior force. They had mobility. By dawn they could put men up on the rim of the narrows, and could already have sent more men to the upper canyon. Jerd had to count on that. Namacho was no mere painted savage. He had been tutored in the legends of the past. He had learned through his own experiences in an expedition below the border. He had the native cunning of his own people. He wouldn't do anything foolish, or over-reckless, but he wouldn't back away from a fight even though it might be costly. Probably, in gaining the narrows, the settlers here had tricked the Indians, but one trick wouldn't end the struggle.

The sky grew brighter. It changed from grey to blue. The shadows of the night crept into the earth. Up on the south rim of the narrows Jerd saw three figures. They crept to the edge, peered down, but Jerd and his companions were under a leafy covering, hard to see. Then some movement must have been detected, for an arrow streaked toward them. It curved slightly with the wind and struck the earth several yards ahead. Another arrow followed, then another. This time, an allowance was made for the wind, but it wasn't enough. A dozen arrows were wasted before the Apaches realized they couldn't master the trajectory.

"Those up on the rim ain't no problem," Vanderveer decided. "But what's holdin' up the main attack? Sun must be up over the barrens."

"Just keep patient," Jerd answered. "We'll hear from the main band, soon enough. Have you noticed there aren't any birds around?"

"What does that mean?"

"We're here, under the shrubbery. And up ahead of us, the Apaches are working this way. Any sensible bird would realize that this isn't a normal situation."

"I don't care how they creep," Vanderveer said. "When they come over the trail, they got to come one behind the other."

"But so close together, it'll be a job to stop them. When they come pouring in . . ."

A screaming cry announced the attack. Bounding down

the trail came one of the Apaches. Two bullets dropped him, but following the first Indian was another, then another. Jerd fired his rifle almost methodically and beside him Vanderveer did the same. From across the trail, Mike Foss and Lou Carling kept their rifles busy.

That sharp, desperate fight at the narrows couldn't have lasted very long but the yelling and the blasting rifle fire echoed between the sheer, rock walls, intensifying the clamor. Four or five of the Apaches died quickly, partially choking the trail. But more followed them, leaping over their bodies and swinging to either side where the defenders were crouching. A badly wounded Indian sprawled across Jerd's body, temporarily silencing his rifle. He rolled the man aside, finished him with his knife, then emptied his rifle against the Indians still charging the trail. Not far away, Bern Vanderveer was rolling from side to side in a grim struggle with one of the Apaches. Across the trail Mike Foss was shouting profanity and now was using his holster gun.

Then, quite abruptly, the attack ended. At one moment there were leaping figures on the trail. In another, Jerd could see none. But choking the way were the sprawled bodies of the Indians who had been dropped. Some undoubtedly were dead. Some were moving, crawling back. A few of them groaned.

Jerd took a deep, shaky breath. He knew that if the Indians had pressed the attack, in a few more minutes they might have gained the narrows. But perhaps Namacho didn't know that. He had made an experimental attack. He might follow that up with another, or he might have something else in mind.

Beside him, Bern Vanderveer half sat up. A moment before, he had ended his struggle with the Indian who had attacked him, and had thrust his body away. Now Vanderveer spoke and he sounded terribly tired. "Stopped 'em, didn't we?"

"At least we stopped their first attack," Jerd said.

"Seems like a man never learns enough," Vanderveer said. "Whipped that Injun. Thought he was dead. But just afore I rolled him aside, he got me in the back with his knife. Want to see how bad it is, Galway?"

Jerd whipped a look in that direction, then he crawled

closer to see the stab wound through Vanderveer's back.
It looked deep and was bleeding quite heavily. It surprised him that Vanderveer could even speak.

"A scratch," Jerd said, lying. "I'll put a pack over
it."

The man shook his head. "Won't help much, will it?
Am I finished?"

"Never—as long as we can hold out."

"But I won't hold out very long. I can feel it. Gettin'
dizzy, light-headed. Think I'll lay down for a minute."

Jerd bit his lips. He had ripped some cloth from his
shirt and had wadded it over the wound but he knew
the pack wouldn't help, even if he could keep it in place.
There was a bloody froth on Vanderveer's lips.

He wondered suddenly about Carling and Foss and
he peered across the trail. He shouted, "Carling—Foss
—you all right?"

"I'm in good shape, not a scratch," Foss answered.
"But Carling got a spear through the chest. Pinned him to
the ground. Reckon he never knew what hit him. It
was that fast. How about you and Bern?"

"He's been wounded," Jerd answered.

"What about Sam?"

In the excitement of the attack, Jerd had forgotten
about Sam Rogell. Now he looked to where he had been
lying but the man wasn't there, nor anywhere in sight.

From across the trail Foss shouted, "Sam! Hey, Sam,
where are you?"

He got no answer and now, as Jerd reviewed what he
could remember of the Indian attack, he didn't recall
having heard Rogell's rifle. Of course the man might have
been hit and, as a result of the pain, he could have
crawled away somewhere. But that didn't sound very
reasonable. It was more likely that Rogell had scampered
away the moment the Indians appeared. If he had fled
he might still be around but more likely he was racing
up the trail in the direction of the caves.

"Where the hell is he?" Foss demanded. "Was he hurt?"

"Don't know about that," Jerd answered. "At least,
he's not where he was."

"You mean, he ran out on us? Headed up the canyon?
The dirty son-of-a-bitch!"

Jerd smiled crookedly. Of course they might never escape the Apaches, but if they did, and if a split developed between Rogell and Foss, it might work to his advantage. Then he remembered what had happened to Lou Carling, thought of Martha and the baby and recalled her words, begging that he look after her husband. He hadn't done a very good job. If he did manage to get to the caves it wouldn't be easy to face Martha.

The sun climbed higher. It slanted down into the canyon, bright and warm. From where Jerd was crouching he could count seven Apaches slain in the attack. Probably more had been killed, for he could see only part of the trail. As many more, injured, had crawled away. At any moment there might be another attack but so far it hadn't developed.

Not far away, Bern Vanderveer was lying motionless. He had muttered something a little earlier, his words indistinguishable. Jerd leaned nearer the man, but then drew back. Vanderveer's eyes had rolled open, a glassy film covering them. His mouth had sagged open. Sometime during the last few moments, Vanderveer had died.

Now, guarding the trail, Jerd had himself and Mike Foss—with Ellsworth down on the river. Three men left. If the Apaches attacked again, and in any force, they wouldn't be able to hold the narrows.

He spoke in a low tone. "Foss, can you hear me?"

"Yep. What's on your mind?"

"Vanderveer's dead. That leaves you and me and Ellsworth down on the river."

"You mean we ought to run. I'm in favor of it. Reckon the women have got to the caves?"

"Hope so. How good are you at running?"

"Maybe the Injuns won't be right after us."

Jerd shook his head. "Guess again. Look up at the rim. The Apaches we saw up there earlier are still there. The minute we break from cover, they'll signal to the others below the narrows."

"So it'll be a running fight from here. Can't be helped. Galway, if I don't make it to the caves but you do, take care of Rogell for me."

"Think I should, huh?"

"Damned right."

"Want to tell me about that stage holdup?"

The man laughed coarsely. "Nope. Won't go that far. Might get to the caves, myself."

"And if we do?"

"Why, if we do it all depends. Right now, I'm liable to say anything. But if we slide through this alive, why, I got to think about myself and what's best for me. Rogell's a big man. He's got money to spend. You're living under a prison sentence."

Jerd was scowling. He was angered by what Foss had said. At least, by inference, Foss had admitted he knew something about the holdup—something which hadn't come out in court. But, in spite of the circumstances in which they were caught, he wouldn't talk.

"I ought to throw you to the Apaches," he muttered.

"They'll probably get us anyhow. You ready to run?"

"Yes. I'm ready. I'll cut down to the river to get Ellsworth."

Jerd backed away, stood up and then slanted down toward the river where Ellsworth was hiding. As he did, he glanced up at the rim. The Indians there were waving, probably to those below the narrows. In no time at all they would be followed. It would be a race up the canyon, with death holding the stakes.

Chapter XII

LAURIE STUMBLED ahead. Her body was wracked by weariness. Her arms and face were badly scratched. Both knees were skinned and she had twisted her ankle, which made, her limp. Her throat ached. She was short of breath and she knew she was running a fever. The last time they stopped she had refused to get up and move on, but her father had jerked her to her feet. He had been as gruff to her as when she had been a child and slapped her backside with a force she could still feel.

"We're almost there!" he had half shouted. "Any minute we'll break in the open and see the caves!"

She didn't believe him. She knew they would never

reach the caves but, once again on her feet and urged forward, she kept going.

The sun was well up in the sky and maybe the trail was easier, as Midge had just called encouragingly. It was even possible that the canyon had widened. She could scarcely notice it, however. The fragmentary thoughts which ran through her mind formed no cohesive pattern. And hope for the future had no part in them. They had been led into a trap. Not one would escape.

On either side the screening shrubbery was thinner and now, here and there, she could see huge, lumpy boulders, outcroppings of rocks, some of them overgrown and seemingly held fast by the thickets. Up ahead, however, the boulders were thicker, and even underfoot it was rockier, as though they were following the dry bed of a river.

Her father's sudden, sharp cry startled her. "There they are, the caves, off to the left!"

He was pointing. Laurie looked that way. Across the boulder field was the north wall of the canyon and just above ground level were the dark openings of the caves. She could see three, no, four. And they weren't far away.

A quick surge of hope ran through her body. She had thought they would never make it but she had been wrong. In two or three hundred steps they would be there, at the end of the journey. Safe. And in a fortress they could defend. Behind them George was shouting to everyone to hurry. Others answered his cry. Young Erb Ellsworth gave a triumphant yell. Midge called encouragingly to Martha. Rita started running, cutting off toward the caves alone.

"We've made it," Dan Hale shouted. "In five more minutes . . ."

His voice broke off. He stiffened, clutched at his chest. In his hands he seemed to have grabbed the shaft of an arrow. It had ripped deep. The chipped point of the arrow protruded from his back.

Staring at him, Laurie screamed. She saw her father pitch forward. Ahead of him, not more than a dozen steps away, an Apache had moved in sight from the shelter of a granite boulder. He was short, stocky, his face painted horribly. And, even as Laurie stared at him, the Indian was notching another arrow.

From behind her Laurie heard the blast of a rifle. The Indian, ready to loose another arrow, seemed to jerk backwards. He threw up his arms as he fell but he hadn't been alone. In a sweeping glance, Laurie saw three more, then another and another. They were screaming as they rushed forward and from the sounds they made it seemed to Laurie that the canyon was alive with Indians. She saw two hurling spears. Another was driving straight at her, an upraised knife in his hand. But he didn't reach her. He stumbled as a bullet hit him.

Cutting through all the confusion, George Odlum was shouting orders to them, yelling at them to run for the caves. But Laurie couldn't. She couldn't move. She seemed frozen where she was. Others were heading for the caves, however. Laurie caught a confused picture of what was happening. Rita Dawson, who had started first for the caves, hadn't stopped. She was dodging through the boulder field like a deer, as though not tired at all. Behind her Laurie saw Alice, but, even as she looked, an Indian caught Alice and they both went to the ground. George was racing to help her.

At a nearer point, Martha and Midge disappeared around a boulder and farther away Jane Ellsworth was struggling with one of the Indians. Then, amazingly, Aaron Ellsworth came in sight, rushing to his wife's side. Behind Aaron she caught a glimpse of Jerd and Mike Foss. Jerd turned aside but Mike continued toward her.

"Get on to the caves," he yelled, and he gave her a shove. Then he swung to where Ruth was kneeling at Dan's side and pulled her to her feet. "Get on to the cave," he yelled again. "Only a few Injuns here. We can make it if we hurry, but we got to hurry. There's more of 'em coming."

The last two hundred yards to the caves would always remain in Laurie's mind as a horrible nightmare. She stumbled and fell probably a dozen times and Mike Foss wasn't gentle about getting her up. He cursed her, slapped her, and once he kicked her. He practically carried Ruth, but he seemed to have no respect for Laurie at all. At some future date she might be able to appreciate what he did for her but she would never like him—never fully understand him.

She did make it to the caves, however, and she crawled into the one someone chose. Then, for a time, she just lay there, hardly aware of the others who had reached it—or who hadn't.

Midge struggled weakly, but she was only vaguely conscious of what she was doing. A man was droning words in her ears, whispering over and over, "Stop it, Midge. Lie still. Lie still. And don't make a sound."

He kept saying the same things, and he seemed angry. His arm was across her shoulders like a rigid iron bar, holding her down. There was a pounding pain in her head, an incessant pain that wouldn't let up.

It came gradually to Midge what had happened. As they had turned to the caves, sure they would make it, a number of Indians had appeared to block their way. They had seemed to spring out of the earth and had rushed toward them, screaming horribly. Dan Hale had been killed instantly. And probably others had been killed. As she and Martha had started for the caves she had caught a glimpse of Jane Ellsworth struggling with one of the Indians. Another had been closing in on Alice Boulder.

But that had been all she had been able to see. As she and Martha rounded a huge boulder they had run into three of the Apaches. Two had grabbed Martha, one of them tearing the baby from her arms. The third Indian had plunged toward Midge. She had dodged away, tripped, and plunged to the ground. And as she hit the ground, everything went black.

Probably, Midge realized, she should be dead. But rather strangely, she wasn't. Instead, she was flat on the ground somewhere, a hammering pain in her head. And someone was with her, holding her down and growling at her. A man, but who he was she didn't know.

She tried to shift her position but the man's arm stiffened. He spoke again. "I said, lie still."

She managed a question. "Who are you?"

"Jerd Galway."

"But you were back at . . ."

"We left the narrows. We were racing up the trail.
Got here just as someone screamed and as the Indians
attacked. Lucky for us they were only a small scouting
party. Must have seen you from the rim, then hurried
ahead, found a way down into the canyon, and set up an
ambush."

"Where are we now?" Midge asked.

"Within a dozen yards of where you fell."

"Why don't we go on to the caves?"

"Can't right now. The Indians who chased us up
the trail are all around us. That's why I don't want you to
move. We better not talk, either, even in whispers."

Midge bit her lips. She lay motionless for a time, and
without speaking. But there was one more question she
had to ask even though she was afraid of the answer.
She put it in words. "Where is Martha, and the baby?
Did they—?"

"Don't think about them," Jerd said.

"You mean . . ."

"Just don't think about them."

Midge took a shaky breath. She closed her eyes. Martha and the baby were dead. In the last moments of their
flight and while they were within sight of the caves
where they might have been safe, the Indians had caught
them. She shook her head numbly, not wanting to believe what had happened. A sudden wave of anger swept
across her. Up to this moment she had been frightened
of the Indians. She had fled as one might want to escape
from a plague, aware of no deeper feelings than that.
In the flash of a moment, however, she was changing.
The Indians were no longer a body of men whom she
feared. She could hate them, too. She could hate them
with a bitterness which made her tremble.

Jerd's arm across her shoulders tightened slightly. His
whisper probably was supposed to be comforting.
"Steady, Midge. If any of us live through the next few
days, we'll be lucky."

Tears squeezed through her close-lidded eyes. She
could remember just how the baby felt in her arms. She
could remember how the baby had smelled and cried and

laughed—a heavy bundle but too precious to be measured. She was crying softly.

Jerd spoke again. "Stop it, Midge. If the Indians find
us . . ."

They were under a ledge of rock or, more probably,
under the rounded lower edge of one of the boulders. A
tangle of shrubbery gave them a scant covering. Midge
knew Jerd must have pulled her here after she had lost
consciousness. He had hidden her undoubtedly because
he hadn't had the chance to get her to the caves. He
had said the Indians were all around them. But what of
the others with whom she had fled up the canyon? Had
any made it to the caves? She had to know.

Turning her head she looked at him. "What of the
others?"

"Several made the caves," he answered, whispering.
"Rita Dawson, George Odlum—I think the Ellsworths,
and perhaps Laurie, Ruth and Mike Foss, but I'm not
positive."

"Alice?"

"No, Alice didn't make it."

Midge was silent for a moment, thinking of Alice
Boulder. She scarcely knew her, but that made little
difference. Alice had been a frail, aging woman. What
kind of people were those who made war against women
and children? Dan Hale had referred to them as savages
and that was true.

She spoke suddenly and too loud. "I hate them, hate
them, hate them. I've heard men say before that the
Apaches ought to be stamped out, just like wolves. I
didn't agree, but now I do. If I live . . ."

"You won't if you keep talking," Jerd said. "Save it
for later."

"But I . . ."

Her voice broke off. Her eyes widened as she stared
at the man beside her. What was it that Laurie had told
her about him? *That he was half Indian. The child of an
Apache woman. Reared with the savages who had slain
John and Alice Boulder, Seth Dawson, Dan Hale, and
Martha and her baby!* A sudden revulsion made her
choke and made her sick at the stomach. The touch of

his arm across her shoulders was like a burning brand.
She was suddenly frightened.

"Hey, what's the matter with you?" Jerd whispered.
Her voice was shaky with feeling. "Don't touch me!"

"Huh? What do you mean?"

"Just don't touch me."

He looked puzzled, confused, but he drew back his arm
and then edged away from her so he wasn't pressing
against her. Then he made a caustic comment. "Sorry I
forgot my lessons from *Godey's Lady's Book*. I'll try to
be more proper."

Midge looked away. For an instant she disliked
herself, for she wasn't a prissy person. Then she thought
of Martha and the baby and her lips tightened. She
hated everything that was Apache, or even half Apache.
Lying rigidly at his side, she tried not to think of him.

From the direction of the caves, Jerd heard the blast
of a rifle shot, then another and another. For five minutes, possibly, the firing continued. After that it stopped,
and since he heard no wild shouting on the part of the
Apaches, he knew the defenders still held the cave. He
couldn't see what was happening and he couldn't risk
a look, but it was easy to guess what was going on. The
Indians, as yet, had made no direct attack on the cave,
but from here and there in the rocks they were using
their arrows, pinning the defenders inside, drawing
their fire.

Jerd peered out at the shadows made by the sun. It
probably was just after noon. That being the case, he and
Midge faced long hours of waiting. When it got dark, they
could try to reach the caves—but that was looking far
ahead. With the Indians all around them, at any moment
a prowling warrior might stumble on their hiding place.
If that happened, he and Midge wouldn't last very long.
He could be sure of that.

He was scowling. He didn't like this situation at all but
there wasn't anything he could do about it. The Indians,
chasing him, Ellsworth, and Mike Foss up the canyon,
had been terribly close behind them. And after he
reached Midge, and found she was still living, he hadn't
had the chance to get her to the caves. Unconscious, a

dead weight, he couldn't have lugged her through the boulder field before the Indians overtook them. He had had to find a place to hide.

The girl beside him stirred. She looked at him, then quickly looked away. Jerd stared at the back of her head, puzzled about her attitude. Of course, he didn't know her at all but, from what he had seen of her in her uncle's home in the canyon and his few glimpses of her throughout the trip to the narrows, he had been impressed by her courage, her self-assurance, and her level-headed judgments. She scarcely knew this frontier country, but her first reactions to the Indian attack hadn't been to get hysterical or go to pieces. Instead, she had met the test with superlative stubbornness. But then, what had happened to her in the last few minutes? What had frightened her? Or more accurately, what had made her frightened of him?

He had heard no one near them. If they kept their voices low he didn't see why they shouldn't talk and now he spoke to her again. "Midge, what's wrong?"

She shook her head. "Nothing."

"But something is. You've changed."

She was silent for a moment, then she asked, "How many of you escaped from the narrows?"

"I did, Aaron Ellsworth, and Mike Foss."

"What happened to the others?"

"Bern Vanderveer and Lou Carling were killed by the Indians."

"And Sam Rogell?"

"I don't know what happened to him. He disappeared —fled up the canyon ahead of us. Or at least I think he did. He should have caught up with you."

"But he didn't."

"Then I don't know where he is."

She turned to look at him. "You hated him, didn't you?"

"At least we weren't fond of each other."

"You could have killed him."

"I didn't."

"You're one of them, aren't you?"

"One of them?" Jerd repeated slowly. "Now, just exactly what do you mean by that?"

"You're half Indian."

His voice sharpened. "Who told you that?"

"Do you deny it?"

"Sure, I deny it. I was captured by the Indians when I was about two years old. My parents were as white as you."

"That isn't what I've heard."

He was suddenly angry. "Then think what you wish. If it'll make you feel any better, believe I'm half Indian. What difference does it make?"

They fell silent. Jerd turned on his side away from the girl and he was careful not to touch her. To hell with her, anyhow. Let her be frightened, if that was what she wanted. Just so she was quiet, and could endure the long afternoon. After it got dark, he would try to get her to the caves. Once that was done, she could avoid him completely.

He heard another intermittent burst of rifle fire from the direction of the caves, but it didn't last long. The Indians apparently weren't ready for a direct attack. Or perhaps Namacho hadn't arrived. He would have stayed with the main body of the Indians and their extra horses and he probably was still up on the rim.

He grinned crookedly, thinking of Namacho. Already, the raid on Eden canyon had cost the Apaches more men than they could afford to lose. More time, too. And the engagement wasn't over. Namacho would be wise to desert them and strike somewhere else, but Jerd didn't think he would. To wipe out his losses, Namacho needed a victory, and, so long as the defenders held the caves, he couldn't boast of his accomplishments. Right now, unless he was badly mistaken, Namacho was a bitter, unhappy man.

Chapter XIII

THE LONG AFTERNOON spent its weariness. The sun dropped from sight. Night shadows crept from the earth, grew thicker, more dense. The constant wind, warmed from the sands of the barrens, swept across the boulder field, rustling the scanty shrubbery, whispering around the rocks. In the sky there were clouds, black and threatening. Jerd couldn't see them from where he and Midge were lying, but he could sense their presence. At any hour, it might rain.

Jerd had dozed for a time and he had needed it. Midge might have done some sleeping, too. At least she had been very quiet. They had scarcely talked. But it was time to talk now, for their trip to the caves might not be easy.

"Be dark in a few minutes," Jerd said, his voice low. "When I think we can risk it, we'll start for the caves. Are you listening?"

"I'm listening," Midge answered.

"We've probably got two hundred yards to cover. Maybe the Indians have left, or maybe none will be near. On the other hand, might be fifty of them between us and the caves. Because we don't know what lies ahead, we're going to be very careful. To cover the distance might take us two hours, or even longer. Have you ever crawled on your face?"

"I think I know what you mean," Midge said.

"On your face," Jerd said. "And with your entire body flat on the ground. You edge ahead, inches at a time. I'll go first. You keep your hands close to my feet. If I stop, you stop. When I first get out, I'll stand up, maybe. Then you can, just to flex your muscles. After that, sink to the ground. As you crawl, don't raise your head to look from side to side. And don't get up on your knees, ever. Understand?"

Her voice was sarcastic. "Certainly. I'm not entirely without intelligence."

"It isn't a matter of intelligence," Jerd said flatly. "All the books you ever read won't tell you how to get from here to the caves. I'd feel better if you knew less."

"Or if I was one of the savages."

"I thought you'd get to that. So now they're savages. Hate me if you wish, but the Apaches are a proud race. If you think they're vicious and cruel, look at some of the things we've done to them."

"I would expect you to defend them."

"What I've said was true."

"I can't believe a word you've said."

He was goading her because he couldn't help it, because he had to hit back. His words were bitter. "Sure, I know how it is. White folks are good. Indians are bad. We are Christians, they are heathens. We have honor and believe in justice. An Indian is sly and deceitful. We love our children but an Indian child is neglected and no one loves him. It's a wonderful thing to be white."

He expected a sharp answer, but she surprised him. She said nothing. She was breathing heavily, however, and Jerd knew she was burning with anger.

"I'll give you a little time to calm down," he said gruffly. "And I want to say one more thing before we leave. If the Indians discover us before we reach the cave and if I yell at you, jerk to your feet and run."

Again she didn't speak. Jerd twisted away. He peered into the gathering shadows. It had been getting darker all the time. He couldn't see very far, which could be an advantage or a disadvantage, depending upon what happened. The night would cloak their progress as they crawled forward, but it would also hide the Indians and unless he was awfully careful they could easily blunder into trouble.

"Ready, Midge," he whispered. "No more talking until we reach the caves. Keep close behind me and don't make a sound. Stand up when I motion. After that, get down and keep to the ground."

He didn't wait for her answer. Turning, he edged away then, several moments later, still in the deep shadows of the rounded boulder which had sheltered them, he stood up, listening sharply and looking from side to side, searching the darkness. The stars above them were hidden by clouds. The wind seemed sharper and in it he could sense the possibility of rain. A sudden flash of lightning gave him a glimpse of the boulder field and the stark face of the canyon's north wall. They had to climb slightly to reach the caves but in that brief glimpse it was impossible to chart his way.

Midge, crawling to join him, stood up. A tall, slender girl, but not thin. She had dark hair, but over it she had tied a scarf. Not a bad-looking girl, but the stony expression she had worn all afternoon made her seem older than she was and harder. But for a person new to this part of the country, she had done very well.

Jerd gave her a chance to stretch her muscles but after that he touched her shoulder, then sank to the ground and edged away. Looking back a moment later he saw her on the ground, following him.

Lightning flashed again and this time it brought a rumble of thunder. Jerd crawled on in the direction of the caves but he moved very carefully, slowly. He had been encouraged by the thunder. He wanted to hear more, and then he wanted a driving, drenching rain, but he was afraid he couldn't count on it. Lightning and thunder didn't always bring a rain.

It wasn't an easy trip toward the caves. The earth below his body was hard, bumpy with rocks. Some had sharp, cutting edges. It was hard to make no noise. The rolling of stone against stone couldn't always be smothered by their bodies. In the first half-hour, however, Jerd knew he couldn't complain about his companion. Occasionally, he heard her. If an Indian was lurking nearby, he might have heard her. But all in all, Midge was doing a good job in following his directions.

The lightning flashed again and again. The thunder rolled down the canyon. Rain seemed more likely and for that Jerd was glad. In the last flash of lightning he had caught a glimpse of two Indians, huddled behind some rocks off to his right. If he had seen two, there were more nearby.

They crawled on. Undoubtedly most of the Indians weren't crowded around the caves but, throughout the night, a number would make sure no one could escape and, just as back at the house, there would be a few prowlers hunting for scalps. Jerd had a knife he could reach quickly and a holster gun in his back pocket but he didn't want to have to use either one.

Again it lightened, thundered, and then suddenly the rain hit them, coming first as hailstones, hard and icy, some as large as the ends of his thumbs. They hammered his body like showering pebbles driven from a cannon. Jerd crawled on, glad of the storm, but in a moment he looked back. Damned if Midge wasn't keeping with him, ignoring the discomfort she must be feeling.

The hail slackened, changed to rain—an icy, cold rain. It beat down at them, driven by the wind. In an instant they were soaked through. Jerd kept moving toward the caves, but he was taking advantage of the storm. He was traveling faster. Of course the Indians wouldn't have left. They still would be guarding the caves. But the sounds of the storm smothered other sounds. The storm had become an ally.

The cut in Jerd's arm, tightly bound, had been sealed shut by caked blood. He had been able to feel it constantly but its pain was something to endure. Now, under the driving rain, he could feel the bandage loosening but there wasn't anything he could do about it. And, at least, they were now more than halfway to the caves. So let the arm bleed again, if it had to. If he made it to the caves, he could have it bandaged again.

Jerd peered ahead, then glanced from side to side. Because of the rain and the darkness he couldn't see very far. But he had checked his direction with the last flash of lightning and he thought he knew just where they were. Remaining between them and the caves were a number of huge outcropping rocks, but beyond there the terrain was fairly open. It was rocky land, uneven, and it wouldn't be easy to run across. But when they got that far they were going to have to run. He could think of no way to avoid it. The Indians guarding the caves would be scanning this area from several points. Anyone trying to crawl across it would be detected.

Jerd turned on his side, motioned to the girl and a moment later she crawled up beside him. He leaned closer. "How do you feel?"

"Wet," Midge answered.

He couldn't help grinning. "Just ahead are some big rocks. After we've passed them we won't have any cover. Have to run—and I mean run. Think you can?"

"Yes."

"After you start running, shout your name. Shout it loud, so the folks in the cave know who's coming. After all this trouble, I don't want you shot."

"Just tell me when to start running."

He spoke again. "We're not alone in the darkness. Next few minutes are important. Keep low to the ground as you can."

She nodded as though she understood. Jerd moved on, leading the way. He stopped several times to study the shadows, thicker against the rocks. In the lee of those rocks, somewhere, some of the Apaches were crouching. He didn't want to run into any of them if he could help it. Right now he could have appreciated a flash of lightning, but that part of the storm seemed over. The rain didn't slacken, however. It still hammered at the earth from the black clouds above.

Jerd changed direction, angling to avoid one of the huge rock barriers in the way. He turned again toward the caves, but suddenly stopped. Through the driving, wind-blown rain, he heard the sound of guttural voices, snatches of words he couldn't catch clearly, Apache words. Off there to his right and not far away, were at least two Indians. He stared that way, probing the black shadows. A lumpy figure straightened, probably to peer toward the caves, but then settled down again. Near him, another shadow moved.

He rolled to his side, motioned to the girl. She pulled even with him and, leaning toward her, he whispered, "Straight ahead, Midge. Slow and close to the earth. But be ready to run. It's not much farther."

She didn't answer. She crawled on slowly, scarcely making a sound. But the rain had lightened and now wasn't so noisy. Jerd could hear the two Apaches talking. Their words were still low but he could make out what they were saying. Both were boasting. In the morning, those who had taken shelter in the caves would be destroyed. Namacho had decreed it.

Midge passed him. Still hugging the ground, she moved on and though she was careful, Jerd could hear the sound of her progress and, just as he had feared, the two Indians heard her. One stood up, then the other. They seemed to be staring in her direction.

Jerd drew his gun. On his scouting trip with Ingraham, he had told him that, in an enemy country, the knife was better. To avoid attracting attention, that was true. But a gun was faster than a knife and he had a shelter if he could reach it—the caves. So the weapon to be used now was his gun.

He sighted at the two Indians, heard one of them shout suddenly and draw back his arm to launch a spear. Jerd waited no longer. He could have wanted Midge to be nearer the caves before she was discovered but it hadn't worked out that way. Jerd squeezed the trigger. The Indian, with the spear, collapsed, turning sideways, sprawling on the rocks. Jerd switched his aim. He fired at the second Apache, then raised his voice in a loud shout. "Now, Midge! On your feet. Race for the caves."

He jerked erect as he said that. The Indian who had dropped back against the rocks wasn't finished. A spear hurtled through the air. Jerd sensed its passing. He fired another shot at the Indian against the rocks, then whirled and raced after Midge.

She had whipped to her feet, plunged straight ahead. She was running through the darkness. She was shouting. "It's Midge—Midge and Jerd Galway. Don't shoot— don't shoot!"

Behind them, Jerd heard several Indian shouts. He knew that arrows were streaking past but they were rushing into the deeper shadows of the wall of the canyon. Ahead of him, Midge tripped and fell but she was on her feet again before he caught up with her. And then, finally, he heard the shouts he had been awaiting. "This way, Midge. This way!"

The voice sounded like the voice of George Odlum and in another moment they reached the cave. Someone came out to meet Midge and help her the last few steps. There was no one to help Jerd, but he didn't need it. Following the others inside, he found a place in the darkness to sit down.

There were eleven in the cave, five men, six women. Jerd enumerated them in his mind as he considered what to expect in the morning. The men, in addition to him, were Mike Foss, George Odlum, Aaron Ellsworth and his son Erb. The women were Laurie, her mother, Midge, Rita Dawson, Jane Ellsworth and her young daughter. Fortunately, none were seriously injured. In the defense of the cave everyone here, with the possible exception of Kathie Ellsworth, should be able to help. The chief problem now was the matter of ammunition and how far it could be stretched. If they ran out of bullets, they wouldn't last very long.

Ruth found him in the darkness. She never had been fond of him, but she was one of the few who still called him by his first name and along the trail she had seemed to understand why he had to drive her. Crouching beside him, she spoke of Midge. "We had given up hope of ever seeing her again. I want to thank you, Jerd, that you brought her to the cave."

"She really made it on her own," Jerd answered gruffly. "She's had a rough introduction to the west. How do you feel?"

"Tired, bitter about what's happened. You know Dan was killed? He had no warning that the Indians were near us. It was an ambush."

"It's lucky any of us made the caves."

"But are we safe now?"

"No."

"How long can we hold out?"

He shook his head. "I don't know that."

She sounded weary. "I'm not sure it's worth it to go on struggling. Of course I don't mean that, but so many of us are gone. Dan, and the Carlings, John and Alice Boulder, Rita's husband and Sam Rogell. I suppose Sam was killed."

He didn't know what had happened to Sam Rogell. If he had fled up the canyon, he should have caught up with the others. Since he hadn't it was quite possible he was dead.

Someone had joined them in the darkness. From her voice it was Laurie, and her question was almost an accusation. "Jerd, what happened to Sam Rogell?"

"I'm not sure, Laurie," he answered honestly.

"I talked to Mr. Ellsworth," Laurie said. "He didn't see what happened at the narrows. He said he was guarding the river. I asked Mike Foss, but he said he was across the trail from you and Sam. He couldn't see, either."

Jerd felt a sudden, stirring anger. Certainly, Mike

Foss could have said more than he did. After the Indian attack at the narrows, Rogell's body at least wasn't found. And he had advocated fleeing up the canyon much earlier. Jerd was sure Rogell had tried it, but he didn't know how he could prove it.

"Back at the narrows, Rogell, Vanderveer, and I were below the trail," he said slowly. "When the Indians hit us, we were busy. For several minutes I didn't have a chance to look to either side. Then, after the Indian attack was broken, and when I could look around, Rogell was gone."

"Gone where?" Laurie asked.

"I don't know."

"But where could he have gone?"

"Up the canyon."

"You mean—he ran away? But Sam wouldn't have done a thing like that."

Jerd was silent. He felt suddenly weary of defending himself. He was sure in his own mind that Sam Rogell had run away but he was afraid he would never be able to prove it. It might help if he could say Rogell had tried to make all of them head up the canyon, much earlier. Mike Foss could verify such a charge, but if he wouldn't, the only other witnesses, Lou Carling and Bern Vanderveer, were dead.

"I just can't believe Sam would have run away," Laurie said. "There must be some other explanation."

"Maybe there is," Jerd said flatly. "Maybe we'll find it."

He fingered his wounded arm. It hurt terribly and was bleeding again, but not badly. His clothing was still soggy from the rain. He wondered if he didn't feel almost like Ruth Hale—as though there wasn't much point in struggling on. But a man had to, no matter what the odds, or no matter how empty the victory might be. The effort to survive was as instinctive as the hunger for food—which reminded him he hadn't eaten.

"I could eat something," he said.

"I'll bring some food," Laurie said. But she didn't sound very enthusiastic.

Chapter XIV

THE RAIN SLACKENED, stopped, but clouds still hung in the sky, making the night darker. From just inside the mouth of the cave and from behind a rock barrier which had been erected, Mike Foss pointed up canyon. "Injun camp," he suggested to Jerd. "But where did they get the dry wood?"

"From the lee of the rocks in the canyon," Jerd answered. "From protected places. The Indians often have to contend with rain."

He stared toward the glow of the fire, wishing he could scout it. To leave the cave and to return, however, involved too much of a risk.

"Don't know why they didn't hit us this afternoon," Foss said. "Think they've had enough?"

"I doubt that," Jerd said. "Could be Namacho ran out of daylight before he could attack. He had to move his horses out of the main canyon, ride them here, make a horse camp up on the rim, and then drop down here by foot. We'll hear from him in the morning."

"Wish it was a day later," Foss said. "If it was, the Army might reach us. I been thinking. Yesterday, we didn't hear any shooting down the canyon. Maybe the stagecoach from Wickenburg saw the fire smokes, figured we'd been attacked and turned back. The stagecoach could have got back to Wickenburg—maybe this afternoon. If the Army didn't waste any time, they could get here by tomorrow night."

George Odlum spoke from the darkness behind them. "Sure, the Army might ride to Eden canyon—but they'll never find us here. Galway's got us where we're trapped. The Apaches can take their time, starve us out. We'll never leave the cave alive."

He sounded bitter, angry. Jerd shrugged. "Maybe you're right. Maybe we're dead, George, or very close to it."

"I want to know what happened to Sam Rogell."

"If we're dead, why worry about that?"

"I want an answer, Galway."

"Ask Foss."

"Nope. Don't ask me," Foss said lightly. "All I'm worried about is me—and what happens in the morning. Sam wouldn't have been much help, anyhow. He was mostly talk."

Jerd swung toward him. "Do you think I killed him?"

"Wouldn't have blamed you none."

"You mean Rogell was responsible for the stagecoach holdup."

Mike Foss laughed. "Nope. Didn't say any such thing. Suppose we see what happens. Got to think about myself. If it looks like we're finished and if it means something to you, why I might be able to tell you quite a story."

Jerd felt a sudden lift. "Did you hear that, George?"

"I still want to know what happened to Sam," Odlum answered.

Jerd started to speak, but changed his mind and was silent. He realized, wearily, that right now it would make no difference to Odlum what Mike Foss might say. The holdup of the Wickenburg stagecoach was far in the past. It hadn't affected George, and the truth would make no difference to him. George Odlum was a frightened man. He wanted to blame someone else for his fears and had settled them on Jerd.

The man prodded him. "Well, Galway—I'm waiting."

"Keep waiting," Jerd said harshly. "Hell with you, George."

He swung away, moved deeper into the cave. Just around a corner of the passageway two candles were burning. The food supplies had been stored there and not far away were the embers of a dying fire where supper had been prepared. Jerd knew the nearby coffee pot wasn't empty. He found a tin, poured it half full and took a sip.

In the faint glow of the candles he could see the figures of several of the women. Rita was stretched out on her back, possibly asleep. Ruth Hale lay near her. Jane Ellsworth was on her elbow, leaning over Kathie who was crying softly. Jerd didn't see Laurie but Midge was sitting against the wall of the cave. He could feel her eyes studying him.

Suddenly she stood up, walked toward him and said, "Your arm's bleeding again, Jerd. Shouldn't it be re-bandaged?"

"I feel it should be cut off at the shoulder," Jerd answered, smiling.

"Move closer to the candles and sit down," Midge ordered. "I'll find the bandages."

He did as she suggested. The women who had packed the food had done a little thinking as well as packaging. They had remembered candles, cooking utensils, and bandages. Unfortunately, all the food packages hadn't reached the caves. He and Midge had lost theirs. Probably so had a few of the others.

Midge joined him and for the next few minutes was busy. She caught her breath as she saw the wound, then said, rather ridiculously, "This ought to be dressed by a doctor."

"I'll hunt one up, when I can," Jerd said.

She bit her lips and, briefly, her hands were shaky. Then she got busy again, smoothed an ointment over the wound and reached for the bandage.

"How are you at sewing?" Jerd asked abruptly.

She looked at him, startled. "You mean—"

"The wound ought to be closed. Two stitches would help."

"I—I couldn't do it."

"Any woman can sew a seam. Do you have a needle and a coarse thread?"

"I have a needle and thread, but I—"

"Soak the thread in the ointment. Clean the needle in some soap if you have that, or plunge it in the embers of the fire. Then put in two stitches."

"It would hurt—terribly."

"It's my hurt."

"Jerd, I just can't—"

"Sure you can," Jerd said. "I'll lie down while you get ready. And if I say anything while you're doing your sewing, don't listen."

He turned on his side. The pain was worse than he had expected, but he knew that it wasn't Midge's fault. After she finished he felt very shaky, soaked with perspiration. And for a time the pain didn't let up. Then gradually it did.

Sitting up he grinned and said, "Thanks, Midge. I know it wasn't easy."

"You'll not be able to use your arm in the morning."

"I may surprise you," Jerd said. "Now find a place to rest. No reason to worry until it's light."

The men had rolled up rocks to block the entrance of the cave but Jerd could have wished the barrier was stronger. He talked to Mike Foss, George Odlum, Ellsworth and his son, checking their ammunition. They had less than he had hoped—at an average, twenty shots apiece. If they faced a direct assault on the cave the next morning, they could easily run out of bullets before it was over.

Jerd found a place to settle down for the night near the barrier. He cat-napped through the dark hours but as the sky began to grow light he got up and in the back of the cave started the fire and put on water for coffee.

Jane Ellsworth joined him. She looked tired. She was a thin, middle-aged woman and never had been very friendly. She had the reputation of being a stern, deeply religious person, inflexible in her attitudes and hard on her husband and her children. But Erb had measured up quite well. Kathie, too.

"I can tend the fire, finish the coffee," she offered. "But we don't have much wood."

"Where did you get the wood you have?" Jerd asked.

"Someone must have camped here once. We found a fire circle just inside, and some wood which hadn't been used."

He nodded. "How's Kathie?"

"Sleeping. But she didn't sleep well. Her knees are skinned, and she's scratched on the arms and face. She's frightened—and she's only eight."

"I think you should be proud of her," Jerd said. "And proud of your son."

"He is a good boy, Mr. Galway."

She had always called him Mr. Galway. She had never called him Jerd. How she actually felt about him, he

couldn't tell but he knew it was foolish to worry about it.
The other women were stirring, waking up. Jerd turned
away, walked toward the barrier at the mouth of the cave.

Just this side of it, staring into the grey-purple shadows, were Ellsworth, Erb, George Odlum and Mike Foss.
They stood in a tight group, had been talking in low
whispers, but as he joined them they fell silent.

"See anything out there?" Jerd asked.

"Nothing moving," Odlum said. "You know the Injuns, Galway. Could be they're gone."

"I doubt it," Jerd answered. "Wait for a little more
light."

"Then what?"

"I don't know. We'll have to see."

"What do you mean by that?"

"I mean this," Jerd said slowly. "Indians are no more
predictable than we are. I don't know what they'll do. I
can figure things up, I can make a guess, but I could
easily be wrong."

"Let's have your guess, anyhow," Ellsworth said.

"No. Suppose I set up the picture, then you guess.
There are four things to remember, chiefly. First of all,
Namacho hates the white men and would like us all
killed. Second, an Indian doesn't mind dying in battle.
It is a glorious thing to do. Third, and this is a mark in
our favor, Namacho has lost more men than he expected.
He must have lost close to fifteen around Hale's. He lost
better than a dozen at the narrows. He lost more here
near the cave. He still has a strong band, seventy or
more, but he can feel the loss. Then, fourth, time is on
our side. Namacho wants to finish the job here, then
strike somewhere else. He doesn't want to spend several
days starving us out. The Army might show up."

Foss pushed back his hat. "What do you hope, Galway?"

"I've hoped, since we thought of the caves, to be able
to hold out."

"If we had more ammunition . . ."

"But we don't, so we've got to save every shot we can.
I believe this—if we can hold out this morning we'll be
safe. Namacho can't stand many more losses, and he

can't stay here. 'Course, I could be wrong. That's why I said we'd have to wait and see."

The sky was growing lighter but the ground shadows were still heavy. It would be another hour before they could see through the boulder field clearly. Down and up the canyon the thick shrubbery was still hidden in the darkness. Above the south rim the sky looked clear, as though it would be a bright morning.

Laurie and Midge came from the rear of the cave, bringing tins of coffee, and Laurie told them, "Breakfast is almost ready, but it will be a strange breakfast, warm beans and peaches."

Jerd leaned against the barrier. He peered into the early shadows, watching for any sign he could find that the Indians were still here. But he saw nothing. Far off to the left were several pools of water, the headwater springs of Lost river. Beyond and under the trees, the Indians had camped the evening before, their location marked by the glow of their fire. Of course they might have left—or, right now, they might be creeping toward the cave. The pressure of waiting was beginning to tighten his muscles.

Midge brought him a plate of food and then asked, "Jerd, how is the arm?"

"Better."

"I don't believe it."

He smiled faintly. "Honestly, it's better. I can feel it, of course, and I will for several days—but if I save it I will owe it to your sewing."

Foss touched his arm. His voice had sharpened. "Hey, Galway—look out there."

For a moment, Jerd had turned to look at Midge. Now he swung his head to stare outside, and off across the springs he saw a group of the Indians. Possibly a dozen. They had come from the trees, several carrying rifles, the others spears or bow and arrow. One had tied a white cloth to his spear and was holding it above his head.

Jerd studied the group. He was surprised to see the white truce banner. The Indians didn't often use it. Something else, however, startled him much more. In the group walking toward them was a prisoner, a bound figure, supported by two of the Apaches. A white man, heavy, thick-bodied, around his head a bandage. From this distance Jerd couldn't see the man's features. But he didn't have to. He could guess instantly who the man was. *Sam Rogell!*

Odlum also recognized him. "That's Sam," he muttered. "The Injuns have got him."

"Damned if they haven't," Foss said.

They were silent for a moment, watching the Apaches and their prisoner. Rogell's body sagged between the two Indians supporting him. His head drooped forward. His arms were roped against his body. His feet were free but he was dragging them. He might have been conscious. With the Indians was Namacho. He was limping but didn't seem otherwise hurt.

Odlum swung suddenly to Jerd. "How did the Injuns get him? That's what I want to know."

"I don't know," Jerd answered.

"You sure of that?"

Jerd glanced at the man. Odlum's face had tightened. His eyes were hard, angry. He was breathing heavily. Jerd said, "All right, George. Let's have it."

"I'm asking you again how the Injuns got their hands on Sam Rogell. You said he disappeared during the attack at the narrows. Then how did he get here?"

"I don't know, George."

"Maybe Sam disappeared because you hit him over the head and left him to be picked up by the Injuns."

Jerd had a sharp answer on his lips but he held it back. Odlum's accusation was ridiculous. Surely the man couldn't believe it. Jerd stared at him, then glanced at the others. Aaron Ellsworth was watching him closely. Erb looked bewildered. Foss seemed mildly amused but that wasn't strange. Foss didn't really care what happened to Rogell. He was interested only in himself.

Odlum spoke again. "I'm waiting to hear what you say."

He shook his head. "George, you're wrong. And you're not thinking. If you want to raise an issue with me, put it off until we've handled the Indians. Then do your damnedest."

"By God, I'm going to get at the truth," Odlum said angrily.

"Good. I'll help you," Jerd said, and turned again to look toward the Apaches.

They had rounded the springs and were moving closer, Namacho and seven warriors, and two more to support their prisoner. The left leg of Namacho's snagged trousers had been cut off at the knee. Below it, and around his calf, was a bandage. He must have been scratched by a bullet. It wasn't serious for he wasn't limping badly. His face was freshly painted, too—an indication that his raid wasn't to be terminated.

When the Apaches were within thirty yards, Jerd decided they were close enough. Raising his voice, he shouted in their own tongue. "That is close enough, Namacho. Why have you come to us under a white banner?"

"Two days ago," Namacho answered, "we rode to the Canyon of the Buzzards. It has been defiled by the white men. But our work has been done. The Canyon of the Buzzards has been cleaned by fire. This I have done in the name of our people. And in other places will I do other things. I, Namacho, the Chiricahua."

He was boasting, now. In his speech he was parroting other chiefs. Jerd shrugged. "Say on, Namacho."

Odlum touched Jerd's arm. "Make him talk our lingo. I want to know what's going on."

"He hasn't said anything yet," Jerd answered. "I'll tell you when he does."

Namacho gestured with his arm. "We have been delayed a full day by those who fled up the canyon. It was a ridiculous flight, for if we wish it, not one of you will escape. Your lives are mine. But the lives of a few white people are not important. Tomorrow we must meet with some of our brothers of the Mimbres. It is a long journey to the meeting place."

"Then ride on, Namacho," Jerd suggested.

"We would like to do that," the Apache nodded. "We would ride away now, but we are encumbered by a prisoner. We would like to return him to you, but we can do this only in return for one of you—one who belongs to us, for once he was an Apache. He must ride with us when we leave."

"You are speaking of me, Namacho?"

"Yes, Tajawan—who once was my brother."

"How far would I be permitted to ride?"

"How far a man rides is a matter determined by the gods."

"Or by you."

"It is true that men are instruments of the gods."

"And what of the people here, Namacho?"

"They must surrender their rifles and ammunition, but beyond that they will not be harmed."

"Without ammunition and their rifles, you could slay them easily."

"But if I, Namacho the Chiricahua, say that they will be unharmed, then they will be unharmed."

Odlum interrupted again. "What's he saying."

"He's making a proposition," Jerd answered. "I'll explain it in a minute."

Sam Rogell, sagging between the two Indians, seemed to awaken. He raised his head, struggled weakly, then a hoarse cry broke from his throat. "Help me! Don't let them kill me. You don't know . . ."

He didn't get to finish. At a word from Namacho, one of the other Indians struck Rogell sharply over the head with the barrel of a rifle. That knocked him unconscious again.

Behind Jerd, in the cave, one of the women gave a sympathetic cry. It was nearly a scream. And at the barrier, Odlum lifted his rifle. Just in time, Jerd grabbed it and twisted the barrel toward the ground. "Stop it, George," he said harshly. "That wouldn't save Rogell."

"What else will?" Odlum snapped back.

Jerd shook his head. "Wait a minute. Namacho's talking again. I want to hear him."

The Apache had raised his arms again. "My patience is short. Namacho is waiting for an answer."

"Give us time to talk things over," Jerd suggested.

"The time when we must ride is near."

"Give us until noon."

"No. Listen to Namacho the Chiricahua. He will hold back his warriors until the sun comes up—but no longer.

Before then, if any of you wish to live, send out him
who once was an Apache and let him bring with him the
rifles and ammunition of the white men. In return, we
will send our prisoner to you and then will hasten on our
way."

"And if we do not agree, Namacho?"

"Then all who have taken refuge in the cave will die."

Jerd shook his head. "Your reasoning isn't straight.
How can Namacho ride to meet the Mimbres, but still
continue the fight in the canyon?"

The Apache waved his arm. "Namacho the Chiricahua has no more to say. We will await the rising of the
sun."

Turning, the Indians started away, dragging Rogell
with them and at the barrier, just within the cave, Odlum
swore. "They're taking Sam with 'em. We'll never see
him again unless—Aaron—Mike—we could nail every
Injun in sight if we . . ."

"They're still under a flag of truce," Jerd said.

"What the hell does that mean to an Injun."

Ellsworth raised his rifle but then lowered it, shaking
his head. "We can't do it. If we can't respect what we
believe, what's the point in living?"

Odlum sucked in a deep breath. He turned toward Jerd.
"All right, what did they say?"

"They want to trade Rogell for me."

George Odlum didn't hesitate for a moment. "I'm
for it."

"But that's only part of it," Jerd said. "They demand
that we surrender our rifles and ammunition. If you do
that, Namacho said you would not be harmed."

"You mean, if we trade you for Rogell and if we
hand over our rifles and ammunition, we go free.
What's wrong with that?"

"Only one thing," Foss said dryly. "Namacho didn't
mean it. If we hand over our rifles and ammunition, we
wouldn't live ten minutes."

Odlum was perspiring. He licked his lips. "How do you
know he didn't mean it? What if he did? Aaron, what
do you think?"

"I don't think we should give up our rifles," Ellsworth
answered.

"At least we could make a trade—Sam for Galway."
Ellsworth looked away. "I don't like it. But yes, we
could do that."

"Mike, how about you?" Odlum asked.

"You are scared, aren't you?" Mike answered.

"Hell with that. I want to know how you feel."

Mike didn't answer immediately, and Jerd looked that
way. He would wait to hear what Mike Foss had to say,
then he had something to say himself.

"It's like this," Mike said. "If we . . ."

Jerd stopped listening. He tried to jerk around toward
George Odlum and he ducked, sensing the blow that was
coming. But he couldn't escape it. Something smashed
against his head and a smothering pain seemed to swal-
low him.

Chapter XV

WHEN JERD slumped to the ground, unconscious, the first
one in the cave to say anything was Midge Applegate. She
spoke instinctively, almost without thinking. "Why,
I think that was terrible. Why did you do that, Mr.
Odlum?"

He glanced at her angrily. "Shut up, Midge. Keep out
of it."

"But I won't keep out of it," Midge said. "I don't care
what you think of Mr. Galway. I don't care if he's part
Indian. At least, he warned us of the Apache attack. He
brought us here. He's been . . ."

"You ain't concerned in this," Odlum snapped. "You're
just one of the women."

That made her furious. All her life she had been told
that this was a man's world. A few would concede that
women were necessary but their place in life was relatively unimportant. Women could work in the house.
They could slave in the fields. They bore the children.
But they had no voice in anything else. All vital decisions
were made by the men. That was the custom and perhaps
it was wrong to challenge it. Midge looked at the other
women, hesitated, then her lips tightened and she

spoke again. "I think everyone here is entitled to an opinion. My life is as important to me as yours is to you. I think . . ."

"Do you want to see Sam murdered by the Injuns?" Odlum asked harshly.

"Certainly not," Midge said. "But I don't want to see Mr. Galway killed, either. And I don't think you have the right to decide between them. Only God can do that. And you're not God."

"You just keep out of it," Odlum said and he glanced at Ellsworth. "Get something and tie Galway's hands."

Ellsworth glanced over the barrier. "The Injuns are gone."

"We'll call 'em back."

Mike Foss broke in. "There's something else to think about, Odlum. We're not givin' up our rifles, are we?"

"We certainly are not," Odlum said.

"Then maybe we got a fight on our hands an' if that's the case, I'd pick Galway over Sam."

"What the hell do you mean by that?"

"I'm talkin' plain sense," Foss said. "From what we could see of Sam, he was in rotten condition—couldn't help us much. Galway's got a bum arm, but he can still fight. We need him—more than Sam."

"I thought you worked for Sam. I thought you'd want to save him."

"Odlum, I want to save myself," Foss said bluntly. "That comes first. If it comes to pickin' between Galway and Sam, why I pick Galway because he can help me. Sam couldn't. Even if he was in shape he wouldn't be of much help. Sam's mostly talk."

Odlum didn't seem to know what to say in answer and, as he hesitated, Midge took another good look at Mike Foss. He was tall, thin, had a narrow face—tight-skinned, hungry. Without his whiskers and if he had been smiling, he might not have been unattractive, but his eyes were too bold, his lips too thin. He might have been thirty-five, or even forty. Midge didn't feel she knew him, although his reasons for saving Jerd Galway had been quite self-revealing.

Odlum finally found some words which suited him.

"I know your kind, Foss, and I don't like you. I don't know why he hired you."

"He needed me," Foss said, and laughed.

"Hell with you," Odlum said. "I'll handle Galway myself."

He set his rifle against the barrier, started toward Jerd but suddenly stopped and Midge, watching them, saw that Foss had drawn his holster gun and was pointing it at George Odlum.

"You can stop right there," Foss said, and sounded as though he meant it.

Odlum stopped. He took a shaky breath, then raised both fists. "Foss, if you don't . . ."

"Forget it," Foss said. "In the fight that's ahead, Galway's a better man than Sam. That's all there is to it. Back away and leave Galway alone. He's comin' to."

Midge dropped her eyes to Jerd. She heard him groan. He rolled over, then sat up and held his head. In the shadow of the barrier Midge couldn't see his face or his expression, but perhaps he wasn't badly hurt.

"Drag yourself on your feet, soon as you feel like it," Foss said. "Odlum had some notions a while back, but he's changed his mind. How soon do you think the Injuns will show?"

"You know as much as I do," Jerd said thickly.

Midge turned away. She walked to where Laurie was standing and sat down. She knew Laurie would have disapproved of what she said a few minutes before but, fortunately for herself, Mike Foss had stepped forward and taken the center of the stage. That made her defense of Jerd less noticeable.

Laurie dropped down beside her. Her whisper was shaky. "What will they do with Sam?"

She shook her head. She didn't know. She was suddenly afraid they would never see Sam again. He would be slain by the Indians. Then, afterwards, part of the blame for his death could be charged to her. *For she had made a choice between the two men. She had done what she had told George Odlum no one had the right to do.* She was aghast at the part she had taken. She hadn't meant to do it. She had spoken without thinking, shocked at what Odlum had done.

Laurie bit her lips. "Sam will be killed. Jerd will go free. It isn't right . . ."

"We may all die," Midge said.

"No. We can hold the cave. That is, there's a good chance we may. But Sam will be dead."

"Others are dead, too," Midge said. "What about your own father?"

"But that just—just happened."

"And how did Sam get captured? Didn't it just happen that way?"

"We don't know. If Jerd did anything to help the Indians capture him . . ."

Midge shook her head. "I think you're just imagining things. And you say Jerd is half Apache. How do you know? He denies it."

"He's lying."

"Then, what if he is half Apache? It seems to me he's done everything he could to save us."

Laurie raised her head. She stared at Midge, her eyes widening, and drew away. "Yesterday afternoon you and Jerd were together—all alone. What happened between you?"

"Not what you're thinking," Midge answered. She looked away, bit her lips, then quickly closed her eyes to lock in the tears which were forming. In a moment she spoke again. "I will regret that afternoon for the rest of my life. What I did was horrible. I treated Jerd like a leper. If he had done right he would have left me to the Indians."

"My noble cousin," Laurie said sarcastically. "I think you've fallen in love with him."

"I could," Midge said, suddenly defiant.

"Sleep with a half-breed?"

"You thought of it."

"But not after I learned the truth."

"I don't mind," Midge said. "Of course, I think he's white as you."

"You can have him."

"I would have taken him anyhow," Midge said.

"He's a criminal, too. Don't forget about that. He's going back to prison."

"Don't be so sure of that," Midge said. "A prison didn't keep him before."

They fell silent and Midge, staring at the floor of the cave, was amazed at the sudden antagonism which had developed between her and Laurie. But then, from the day she arrived Laurie had resented her, perhaps because they were too much alike and, as the poor, dependent relative, Midge should have been more subservient.

"It's foolish to quarrel," Midge said, making an effort to bridge the gap between them. "If we could forget . . ."

"All I can think of is Sam," Laurie said. "I'll never see him again. We would have—we would have been married."

Her voice broke. She got quickly to her feet and moved away.

Midge started after her but changed her mind. She sank down again and shuddered. Whatever was right or wrong, it was horrible to think of Sam Rogell dying at the hands of the Indians.

Laurie was shaky but more than that she was furious with Midge. Her cousin had become an insufferable person. Her defense of Jerd had been reckless. And she had lied about the afternoon before. She must have. While Midge and Jerd had been hiding from the Indians, something must have happened.

She walked back to the breakfast fire, took a tin of coffee. A sudden regret made her wince. How wonderful it would have been if Jerd hadn't been part Indian. They could have been married. And if Jerd had to go to prison, she would have waited for his return. But such a possibility was out of the question. To live with a half-breed and to bear his children . . .

A sudden revulsion made her hands tremble. Thanks to her father and to Sam Rogell she had awakened to the truth before it was too late.

"Hey, what's wrong with you?" asked a voice at her shoulder.

She looked around at Mike Foss, but even before she turned she guessed who was there. From the time when he came up to her and her mother and hurried them to

the caves, he had seemed to take a proprietary interest
in her. She hadn't encouraged him at all and under
normal circumstances she would have told him promptly
that she didn't even care to talk to him. Because of the
pressure of the Indian attack however, caught in a
situation which was unusual, she had tried to be kind—
democratic.

She tried to smile. "I just thought I'd have another cup
of coffee. How about you?"

He reached to touch her arm, squeeze it. "Why not?"

She twisted away, poured him some coffee and quickly
looked at the others. Her mother and Jane Ellsworth
were looking toward the barrier where the men were
standing. Kathie was with her mother. Midge was staring at the floor of the cave. But not Rita Dawson. Rita
was watching them, and that annoyed Laurie.

"That's mighty good coffee," Foss said.

"It's just coffee," Laurie said.

"Your hands are shaky. They're such pretty hands, too."

"You ought to see them after I've been weeding."

He laughed at that and, looking past him, Laurie noticed Rita still watching.

"You ought to pay more attention to Rita Dawson,"
Laurie suggested. "I know her husband has just been
killed but, before long, Rita will be looking for another
man. She's not destitute, either."

"Any man could get her," Foss said. "A good many
have. Now, as for me, I put my sights higher."

She looked at him directly. "Why didn't you stand
up for Sam?"

"Didn't you hear? Galway can put up a better fight."

"But he's half Indian."

He shook his head. "That's just a story. Sam dug up an
old rumor that wasn't true. He spread it to cut down
Galway's size. You gotta watch Sam."

She didn't believe him at all. A man like Foss couldn't
be trusted to tell the truth.

"Anyhow, Sam isn't much of a loss," he was saying.
"Back there at the narrows where we could have used
him, Sam ran out on us. Sure I worked for him but after
that I don't figure I owe him a thing. Far as I'm concerned, the Injuns can have him."

She bridled at his words. "You wouldn't have said that to his face."

"Yep, I would. You got the wrong slant on Sam Rogell. But maybe he's gonna do us a favor. You like this country?"

She didn't hear his last question. Even though she knew Foss was lying, what he said was upsetting. She felt she had to prove he was wrong, but she didn't know how to go about it.

"Yep, I'm pretty sure you don't like the Territory," he continued. "Don't blame you, 'specially since what's just happened. But I figure maybe that you'd go for Kansas City, or Omaha. Or maybe even Chicago. How would you like to go to Chicago?"

She wasn't interested in going to Chicago. She didn't even want to talk to this man, but she had to be civil. "We still have the Indians to worry about—and it would take a great deal of money to go to Chicago."

"Yep, we got to get away from the Injuns," he nodded. "But we might make it. An' as for the money it would cost, I know where to lay my hands on it. Ten thousand in gold. How does that sound?"

Laurie didn't answer, but she was thinking: *ten thousand in gold. Why that was the amount of money lost in the holdup of the Wickenburg stagecoach. It had been in gold and it never had been found. Was it possible that the money Mike Foss was referring to was the stolen gold?*

"Hey, you don't seem excited," Foss said.

"But I am," Laurie answered. "That would be wonderful. Of course you don't mean it."

He stepped closer. "Why not? Ten thousand in gold."

"I can't believe it."

"You'll believe it when you see it."

She took a deep breath. "Where did you get it?"

He laughed softly. "That would be telling. In a way, I reckon, I earned it. 'Course Sam planned it an' meant to use it himself, but since the Injuns have got him, he won't be around. That means the money goes to us."

"Is it in a safe place?"

"You bet it is. Interested?"

"Yes, I think I am."

He had his hands on her arms. "Then gimme a kiss, to prove it."

"But everyone's looking."

"If you moved back around that rock, no one could see us."

Laurie had to do what he wanted. She needed more information about the missing gold. If she resisted him, he might get angry and refuse to talk any more. She backed away, around the jutting rock and in a minute the man's arms went around her and they were like iron bands. He stooped over her face, his lips found hers and forced them open. His whiskers scratched her face. And as he held her, the full length of her body against his, one of his hands started feeling up and down her back. After a moment of that he shifted his body slightly and his wandering hand came in between them to cup one of her breasts. He wasn't gentle about it, either.

Laurie had stiffened and suddenly she couldn't stand this any more. She strained away from him and thought he would guess how she felt, but apparently he attributed her attitude to the strain of the past two days. He let her draw away but moved his free arm to slide behind her. He spoke thickly. "Say, by God, you're a woman. All woman. We're gonna have a time."

"If we get the money," Laurie said.

"Don't worry about that."

"But what if you get hurt? Shouldn't I know where the money is?"

"It's buried under Sam's house. It's—hey, I didn't mean to tell anyone. You meant it a minute ago when you kissed me, didn't you? You didn't just . . ."

"Kiss me again," Laurie said. "That should tell you how I feel."

This time she couldn't hold back when he kissed her and it was a rough experience. It was like being stripped naked but with her clothes still on. When he finally let her go she was breathless and so shaky she wasn't sure how long she could keep on her feet.

"We can't stay here," she said quickly. "Folks wouldn't understand."

"They'd understand too well," Foss said. "By God, you know I'm almost glad the Injuns showed up."

"You don't mean that. You mean . . ."

She broke off, raised her head and stood listening. Through the thin morning air she heard someone screaming. It seemed far off and the sound faded but then came again, shrill and high. She looked at Mike Foss. "What was that?"

"Must be sunup," the man answered. "Reckon Namacho figgers we're not interested in his proposition. Time to get ready for the attack."

"But the screaming . . ."

"That must have been Sam, bein' tortured. But don't worry about him. He won't last long. No guts."

She heard the scream a third time and she closed her eyes and covered her ears with her hands.

"I better get back to the others," Foss said. "Now listen to me. You stay right there where you can't get hit by an arrow. And don't you worry about me. I'll look after myself."

He kissed her once more, then hurried off and, after she was alone, Laurie leaned against the wall of the cave. When another minute had passed and she heard no more screaming it struck across her mind that Sam was dead.

Someone walked toward her. It was Rita and what she said was like a slap across Laurie's face. "I'm really surprised, Laurie. Have you taken a second look at Mike Foss?"

"You just don't understand," Laurie said.

"I surely don't," Rita said. "Jerd is ten times the man Mike Foss is. If I had a chance at a man like that . . ."

"Even if he was half Indian?"

"You mean you believe that story?"

"Isn't it true?"

"Not a word of it. Seth was in Tucson when Jerd was turned over to the Army by Cochise, after a treaty agreement. There wasn't any question about how he was captured or who his people were. But if you really loved him, that shouldn't have made any difference."

Laurie took a deep breath. Maybe she had been wrong. Maybe she and Jerd . . . She straightened a little and smiled. She had learned something of great value to Jerd Galway. If she used that information wisely it should make up for the way she had treated him the past two days.

Chapter XVI

JERD LEANED against the rock barrier. He stared through the mouth of the cave, studied the boulder field, watching for any sign of the Indians. He knew that, if they used every bit of cover, a considerable number could creep very near without being seen. But a few would make mistakes. As soon as the Indians started closing in, he should know about it.

The lump on his head caused by Odlum's blow still throbbed painfully. It had given him a slight headache. But it could have been much worse and while he had been unconscious almost anything might have happened. Fortunately, he had been saved, and, rather strangely, it had been Mike Foss who had stood up for him. Of course, the man's motives might have been questionable, but he couldn't quarrel with the result.

Odlum had moved to the other edge of the barrier. That put Aaron Ellsworth and his son between Odlum and Jerd—a safe distance. And Odlum had become silent. Even when they had heard Rogell's screaming, Odlum didn't speak. But he turned to stare along the barrier toward Jerd and the tight, ugly expression on his face told how he felt. Odlum hadn't changed his opinions.

Ellsworth had a question to ask with reference to Rogell. "How long will he last, Galway?"

"Not long," Jerd answered. "If they weren't pressed for time, the Apaches could keep Rogell alive, could extend the torture all day. This morning I don't think they will. Rogell's lucky."

"That's a rotten way to put it."

"I'd say that if you'd been caught," Jerd said. "As a matter of fact, I'd give almost anything to save Rogell's life. I'd hoped to prove I was innocent of the stagecoach holdup. With Rogell dead, I can't."

"Hey—look out there," Erb gasped, pointing.

"I don't see anything," his father answered. "What did you think it was?"

"One of the Injuns—way back of the spring. He's out of sight now, behind that rock."

"Must have imagined it," Ellsworth muttered.

"No, he didn't," Jerd said. "I noticed him, too. Aaron, that son of yours has a quick eye. He handles himself pretty well. Some day you're going to be proud of him."

"I don't believe in too much praise," Ellsworth growled.

"If people earn it, why not tell them? Erb, you're doing all right. I'm proud of you."

The boy's eyes flashed. "Thank you, Mr. Galway."

Mike Foss rejoined them. He had been in the back of the cave and returned with a wide grin, laughing softly to himself.

"What's so funny?" Jerd asked.

Foss shook his head. "It wasn't funny. Damn serious matter. But very nice. Very, very nice. What's happening with the Injuns?"

"I think we'll hear from them pretty soon. Erb and I saw one creeping this way. Since then I've noticed two more. Some we won't see until they're quite close."

"Figger they've finished with Sam?"

"Probably."

"Will they charge us—head on?"

"That's what I'd order, if I was leading them. Otherwise it'll be a long process."

"Meant to tell you something," Foss said. "A little while ago you thanked me for taking your side against Rogell. But before then, you had another champion."

"Who was that?"

"The girl who was living with the Hales. Midge Applegate."

Jerd was surprised. "You don't mean it. What did she say?"

"Several things. When Odlum hit you over the head, she jumped right at him. Didn't wait a minute. Told him it was a bad thing he done. Odlum told her to shut up but she didn't. She even said she didn't care if you were part Indian, you had fought for us, brought us here and she didn't want to trade you for Sam. She told Odlum straight. Said he wasn't God."

Jerd looked around to peer into the back of the cave. He thought he could pick out Midge. What Foss had told him gave his spirits a sudden lift. For two days he had felt entirely alone, everyone against him. The people here took his orders, but grudgingly. Such support as he had received had come through selfish interest. No one had seemed to trust him. It was an encouraging thing to find anyone felt differently.

"Keep an eye on things, Foss," he said. "I owe a word with Midge."

He turned and walked toward her and she stood up as he reached her. She looked tired. A tall, slender girl, her face scratched from the trail, her eyes red-webbed, her lips almost without color. She hadn't put up her hair, it hung in two thick braids down her back. Her smile was hesitant. Jerd thought she was going to speak. However she seemed to change her mind and stood waiting.

"I've just heard what you said when I was unconscious," Jerd said. "I'm really sorry I missed listening. Thanks."

"No, don't thank me," Midge answered. "I owed you much more than that. I acted horribly yesterday afternoon. I should have been spanked."

He couldn't help saying, "Should I spank you, right now?"

"People wouldn't understand. But if you want to kick my shins, go ahead."

"How would it be if I saved the punishment for later?"

Her lips twitched. "That will be all right, Jerd."

He liked the way she spoke his name. He liked her honesty, the direct way she looked at him. In fact, if he got to thinking about it, he probably would find a dozen reasons for being interested in her. She was the one who had cared for his arm and who had sewed up the cut. On the trail she had been no trouble and she had carried more than her share of the load. Women used to the frontier might have been expected to face a situation like this but, with very little experience, Midge had adapted herself to the needs of the past two days. You didn't often run into such people.

"Midge, what's going to happen to you?" he asked abruptly.

She shook her head, frowning. "I don't know, really. When my parents died several months ago and I was left destitute, Dan Hale wrote and offered me a

home. I could have married a man I knew but I didn't
love him, so I took my uncle's offer. Now he's dead.
Ruth has a sister in the east. I think she'll go there and
give up her land in Eden canyon. I don't know about
Laurie. And I don't know what I'll do with myself."

"I could make a suggestion," Jerd said. "But it would
be rather foolish. The sheriff is looking down my throat.
He'll want to send me to prison."

"Why let him?"

Her words startled him. "What did you say?"

Her eyes were steady. "If the sheriff was after me and
I was innocent, I wouldn't go to prison if I could help it."

"What would you do?"

"First, I'd try to prove I wasn't guilty. If I couldn't
do that, I'd run. It's a big world."

He suddenly felt reckless. "How are you at running?"

"I'm very good at it."

He took a deep breath. "Would you go with me?"

"Yes."

She hadn't hesitated. Her shoulders had straightened
and her eyes seemed brighter. He could sense the tension
which gripped her. It hit him abruptly that she meant exactly what she said. If he could get away, she would go
with him, even if he had to run—even if he had to live as
a fugitive.

He shook his head, scowling. "A man couldn't ask for
more but I want you to think about it. Running and hiding and running again isn't an easy life and a wandering
trail leads nowhere. After the first few months . . ."

He was interrupted by Mike Foss, shouting, "Hey, Galway! Better get back here. Some of the Injuns have
marched in sight, beyond the spring."

"Be right there," Jerd answered. Then he spoke to
Midge. "We'll think about it."

She shook her head. "I won't change my mind. It's up
to you now, Jerd."

He swung away and, as he started for the barrier,
Laurie called him from deeper in the cave. "Jerd, I want
to see you."

"When I have a chance," he waved. "Stay where you
are, Laurie—out of danger."

He hurried on, scarcely thinking about her. Had Midge

really meant what she had said? But of course she had.
It was impractical, impossible, entirely absurd. A few
days or a week of running would be too much. Or maybe
he was wrong about that. At least, it was a pleasant thing
to think about.

He reached the barrier, peered outside. Just as Foss
had said, a group of the Indians had come in sight at
the edge of the trees and beyond the spring. They might
have numbered a dozen, among them Namacho. At a
guess, the others were his counselors. They stood as mili-
tary officers, looking over a battlefield, there to watch
the progress of the fighting. Namacho was a wily chief.
Undoubtedly, he often led his men in a raid. But he
wasn't leading them this morning—and for a very good
reason. Those who led the attack were going to get killed.

"What do you think, Galway?" Foss asked.

Jerd checked his rifle. "I don't like it. I'm afraid we're
in for a rough time." He raised his voice. "Aaron, Erb,
George—listen to me. When the Indians rush the cave,
hold your fire. Don't start shooting until they're right at
the entrance, where we can't possibly miss. Aim at their
bellies, no higher. A bullet there is damned discouraging.
A shoulder wound doesn't always put a man down."

Two of the women had joined them at the barrier—
Laurie and Jane Ellsworth, each with a rifle. Laurie had
crowded between Jerd and Mike Foss.

"I thought I told you to stay back," Jerd told her.

She flashed him a smile, shook her head. "No. My
place is here."

She seemed suddenly friendly. Jerd thought she was
going to say more, but Mike Foss claimed her attention.
He whispered something to her and she answered him,
but her words were too low for Jerd to catch. He thought
of insisting that she move back, then decided against it.
Laurie could handle a rifle and if the Indians charged
the cave she would be needed. If she stayed well behind
the barrier she might be safe.

"What are they waiting for?" Odlum muttered. "Why
can't they make up their minds?"

Jerd looked outside. At the edge of the trees, Namacho
suddenly raised his arm, gave a shout. At that signal,
half a hundred other voices answered his cry and from

all around them the Apaches jumped in sight from their
hiding places in the rocks. They had crept as close to the
cave as they could. Now, screaming and roaring their
defiance, they hurtled toward the cave.

It was a frightening scene to watch. Jerd couldn't
judge accurately the number of the Indians charging the
cave. There must have been sixty or seventy. It seemed
there were more. The boulder field seemed alive with
them. Short, stunted men, dressed in anything, a few even
in stolen army uniforms. They were bronze-skinned, some
wearing hats but most only a head-band around their
black, shoulder-length hair, their faces streaked with war
paint—white, yellow and red. Here and there Jerd saw
rifles. However, most of Namacho's warriors were
equipped with bow and arrow and spear, and probably
knife and tomahawk. They hadn't been impressive on
horseback. Certainly they weren't on foot. But as fighters
possibly only the Sioux and the Comanches could equal
them.

Arrows were now streaking through the air and into
the cave and Jerd shouted to the others to keep down
and to hold their fire. One man couldn't. George Odlum
cut loose with his rifle. He emptied it and, as Jerd
watched, he saw at least one Indian drop.

"We gotta stop 'em," Odlum screamed as he reloaded.
"We gotta stop 'em before they reach the cave."

In his hurry he dropped the shells he had drawn from
his pocket. And he didn't hunt for the ones he had
dropped, but used others to reload the chamber of his
rifle.

The mouth of the cave was wide enough to admit six
people at a time. That meant that the Apaches couldn't
overwhelm the defenders in a single rush. If Namacho
had had the entire Apache nation at his command, his
warriors could still rush the cave only six at a time—
with six behind and six more behind those. In the next
moment the first six were there. Outside, there must have
been a terrific jam at the mouth of the cave, but the natural law of the situation wouldn't change. To get at the defenders, the Apaches had to charge the cave in a column
no wider than six.

Jerd crouched behind the barrier. With him were Laurie and Mike Foss to his right, and to his left were Aaron Ellsworth, Erb and Jane and, at the far edge, George Odlum—seven crowded close together. Midge and Kathie, Ruth and Rita had been ordered to the back of the cave and around the elbow of the passageway where they were out of the line of fire.

Arrows streaked above them, glanced from the walls of the cave or broke against the barrier. One struck a glancing blow at Ellsworth, drawing a thin, red line across his cheek. Then, as the Indians loomed up at the entrance, blocking the light with their bodies, Jerd shouted an order to start shooting. The crash of rifle fire met the Apaches. Several pitched to the ground and, as the defenders kept firing, more of the Indians went down. But that didn't stop the horde from storming the cave. Pushed on forward by those behind, the Indians moved on. They climbed over their own dead. One who was wounded staggered as far as the barrier and sprawled across it. Another got that far, then another. And still they kept coming.

The screaming and the shouting of the Indians added to the blasting gunfire filled the cave with sound. The acrid smell of the exploded gunpowder burned Jerd's throat. He could feel the sting of it in his eyes. He emptied his rifle, refilled it and emptied it again. But by then the Indians had reached the barrier. A warrior sprawled across it to die but more were behind him.

Jerd knew that, if this kept up, in a few more minutes he and the others at the barrier would be overwhelmed. The pressure of such an attack as this couldn't be turned. The Apaches were paying a heavy price for their victory but it was within their grasp. A hurtling body dived across the barrier straight at Ellsworth and carried him backwards to the ground. Another swept Foss off his feet. Laurie had sunk to the ground, undoubtedly injured, perhaps dead. Odlum, he thought, was still fighting, and Erb, but Jane had sprawled across the body of her husband and the Indian struggling with him.

Only vaguely aware of it, Jerd had stepped back. He had clubbed his rifle and was slashing with it from side to side. He caught one of the Indians in the side of the head,

clubbed at another, and another. There was no time for
thought or for realization. What he was doing now
was instinctive. For the moment there was no Indian
close enough to hit with his rifle, so he dropped it
and grabbed his holster gun. He saw two Indians at the
entrance, snapped a shot at them, then stepped toward
the Ellsworths. Aaron lay motionless and, kneeling at his
side, Jane was pounding at an unresisting Indian, hitting
him over and over.

Jerd took a shaky breath, glanced from side to side.
George Odlum, still on his feet, leaned against the far
wall of the cave just inside the barrier. He didn't seem
hurt. If Jane was injured it wasn't apparent. And Erb was
still on his feet, trembling, tears streaking his face. Foss
was lying motionless on the ground. Laurie, too. But what
he couldn't understand was that the Indian attack had
stopped. With the victory they wanted right in their
hands, the Indians had pulled back. It was unbelievable
that they had gone this far and then stopped.

Odlum, apparently, had reloaded his rifle. Suddenly
he started shooting, aiming low and across the barrier.
A wounded Apache who had been crawling away jerked
and then collapsed under Odlum's bullet. Another, trying to get up, pitched forward and didn't move again. A
third Apache, on his knees and just outside the cave,
dropped and fell on his face. Odlum was killing the
wounded. He was doing it deliberately, systematically,
muttering profanely with every shot.

Jerd stepped that way. He jerked the rifle from Odlum's hands. "Stop it, George. We'll need those bullets
later on."

"Like hell!" Odlum shouted. "Gimme my rifle. Didn't
you hear the bugle? The Army's here."

Jerd raised his head, listened. He didn't hear a bugle,
but suddenly from out in the canyon he could hear the
spatter of rifle fire. It could mean only one thing. Odlum had been right. Help had reached them—and just
in time. He could understand now why the Indian attack had stopped. If an Army force had dropped down
into the canyon to hit the Apaches from the rear, Namacho had had to break off the engagement at the cave.

"Now, gimme my rifle!" Odlum grated.

"Why?" Jerd asked.

"Why!" Odlum screamed. "You know damned well why. Some of the Injuns ain't dead. I aim to finish 'em."

"You're as bad as they are," Jerd said flatly.

"Injun lover."

Jerd didn't hand back the rifle. He leaned forward, slapped the man across the face, slapped him hard enough to knock him down. Then, turning away, he stared to measure the losses of the defenders.

Laurie wasn't dead. She had a deep scalp wound and was unconscious but not seriously hurt. Aaron Ellsworth, however, had two knife wounds in his side and needed a doctor's attention. Mike Foss was dead. As for the others, aside from a few scratches, no one else had been harmed. In view of the attack they had faced, he had to admit they had done very well.

Jerd should have been pleased, but in view of the death of Mike Foss he wasn't. Foss was his last hope that someone could tell the truth about the holdup of the Wickenburg stagecoach. Someone else of course might know the story but he didn't know who. With the deaths of Sam Rogell and Mike Foss his hopes were also dead.

The firing outside kept up but it seemed farther off, down canyon and up canyon. At a guess, the Apaches had fled, pursued by the Army's forces. And, trapped here, the Indians would be cut to pieces. Namacho's proud warriors had been smashed. In fact it was doubtful if any would escape. Down here in the canyon, and on foot, it was only a matter of time until most would be captured.

Chapter XVII

IT WAS LATE AFTERNOON before Captain Noyes had any time for the survivors rescued from the cave. But, with the Apaches pretty well rounded up, he took the time to ask for a report.

"We've set up a temporary camp for 'em," Sergeant Wynant told him. "They number ten. Two children, five

women and three men. Several have slight wounds and
one of the men is badly hurt. The doctor's looking after
him."

"Ten, huh? It's amazing anyone escaped from the
main canyon. And how they got up here, I'll never know.
They put up a terrific fight before we got here, too. I
want to see them."

The sergeant scowled. "Then I suppose I might as well
tell you who's with 'em."

"Yeah? Who is it?"

"Jerd Galway."

"Galway! So that explains it."

"I'd reckon it does. Cap'n, what are we going to do
about Galway?"

"What we've got to do," Noyes said gruffly. "You
know the regulations."

"It don't say in regulations that we got to make a civil
arrest."

"But it's our policy to cooperate with civil authorities,
and you know it. We were specifically asked to pick up
Jerd Galway if we found him—and it seems we have."

The sergeant's voice was bitter. "Sure. Galways joins a
bunch of folks, fights for 'em, keeps 'em alive, and how
do we thank him? By putting him under arrest. That's a
hell of a thing to do."

"That's enough, sergeant," Noyes said sharply. "Tell
Galway I want to see him."

He paced restlessly as he waited. He knew Jerd Galway, he rather liked him. What he faced now wasn't
pleasant. Up to the last few moments he had been very
gratified at the way things had worked out. He had been
crossing the barrens, on a patrol, and by chance had met
the fleeing stagecoach. This had directed him to Eden
canyon. His scouts had picked up the Indian trail, up
the canyon's rim. At dawn he had surprised the Indians
guarding the horses and, a little later, had dropped into
the canyon to engage Namacho's forces attacking the
defenders in the cave.

The resulting action had smashed the Indians. Namacho was dead. More than thirty of his warriors had been
captured. Many more had been killed. It was true, of
course, that most of those killed had been slain by the

settlers, but it would go to his credit that he had saved
the survivors and that he had put a quick end to this
Apache uprising. This was all to the good and might earn
him a promotion, certainly a commendation, and he
would like to end the report right there. Unfortunately,
he couldn't. With the sweetness of victory he also had
run into a job which didn't please him—the necessity of
putting Jerd Galway under arrest.

But he had to grin as he met him and he put out his
hand. "Hello, Galway. You folks must have put up a hell
of a fight."

"We were rather busy," Jerd said. "You got here just
in time."

"How did you happen to be in Eden canyon?"

"I suppose I went there deliberately. I was up in the
Mesquite hills. Ran into a man you knew. Clem Driggs."

"We threw him out of the Army. He turned bounty
hunter. The rumor around Wickenburg was that he was
after you."

"I imagine he was," Jerd nodded. "But before he
found me he murdered an Indian, sliced off his ears. I
made a prisoner of him, but before I could decide what
to do with him, some of the Indians caught us, one of
them Namacho. They took Driggs off my hands."

"Killed him?"

"Yes. They had named him the Ear-robber."

"No great loss to the world. How did you get away?"

"Namacho and I were blood-brothers. He knew I was a
fugitive and he thought I might join him. That's how he
happened to tell me about his plans to raid Eden canyon."

"So you got away and rode to warn them."

"I had an ulterior motive. I wanted to save Sam Rogell's
life. I think he was responsible for the holdup of the
Wickenburg stagecoach, for which I was tried."

"The Indians killed him. We found his body."

"Yes, I know. And with his death went my chances
of proving I was innocent. Another man might have
helped. Mike Foss. But he's dead too. Tell me about Namacho. Is he one of your prisoners?"

"No. Namacho is dead. We've identified his body."

Jerd nodded soberly. With the death of Namacho and
the smashing defeat of the Apaches in Eden canyon, for a

time at least they would have peace in the Territory. That much had been accomplished.

"You know what I've got to do, don't you?" Noyes said, scowling.

"I can guess," Jerd shrugged.

"I have to place you under arrest. Hate it like hell. You ought to get a medal, but regulations don't provide for it."

Jerd laughed. "Do I get tied up?"

"No, we won't have to do that," Noyes said. "But I'll have to separate you from the others, and place you under guard. We'll make it as easy on you as we can."

Captain Noyes kept busy until after dark. He visited the other survivors briefly, checked the security of his prisoners, listened to reports from his patrol leaders, some of whom had just returned from scouring the canyon, searching for additional Indians and, at a make-shift desk, did some necessary paper work by lantern light. He was interrupted in this by Sergeant Wynant.

"Woman here to see you," the sergeant said. "She's one of the survivors."

"Bring her in," Noyes nodded.

The woman who appeared at his desk was tall, slender, young, and, although the strain of the past three days showed on her face, she was damned attractive. She had a bandage around her head. He had noticed her before, had learned her name was Laurie Hale, and been told that her injury wasn't serious. Always responsive to a good-looking woman, Noyes got quickly to his feet, bowed and said, "Miss Hale, what can I do for you? Just name it. The Army is at your service."

"I wish it was," Laurie said. "I've just learned that you've arrested Jerd Galway. I think that was a terrible thing to do. We'd all be dead if it hadn't been for him."

"I know that's true," Noyes said. "And if the Army can help him in any way . . ."

"I'd like to see him," Laurie interrupted.

"Certainly," Noyes agreed. Then he raised his voice. "Sergeant Wynant, bring Galway here."

"I'd like to see him alone," Laurie said.

"That can be arranged, but my tent is a better place than the guard tent. Why don't you sit down?"

She did. Then, looking up, she said, "Captain, I have heard you found the body of Sam Rogell. I don't suppose you know how the Indians captured him."

"As a matter of fact, we do," Noyes said. "Or at least, we have a story. One of our scouts, an Apache himself, has been interrogating the prisoners. Rogell was caught late last night, back near the narrows. Apparently he hid until he thought all the Indians heading up the trail were gone—then he tried to slip back into the main canyon where he might have been safe."

"He must have been trying to get help for us."

"That's entirely possible. How is Mr. Ellsworth?"

"He's resting easier. The doctor doesn't think he's in danger."

"That man Odlum . . ."

"The wrong people were killed," Laurie said. "I wish . . ."

She broke off as Sergeant Wynant entered. He looked excited. He cried, "Cap'n, he got away. Galway's escaped!"

"That's impossible!" Noyes gasped.

" 'Fraid it ain't, Cap'n. Some woman helped him. I ain't got all the details, but she's gone too. Want to send a patrol after them. If you do, you ain't got no time to lose."

"Which woman helped him?"

"The young one. Think her name was Applegate."

As startled as he was, Noyes couldn't help but notice the agitation Laurie felt. She had come to her feet and was breathing heavily. She was pale too, and unsteady. Her eyes had widened.

Sergeant Wynant cleared his throat. "About that patrol . . ."

"No, we'll not send anyone after them," Noyes said slowly. "Our first responsibilities are to the Apaches we've captured and the survivors here. We don't have the manpower to send a patrol after Galway and his companion."

"What—what will happen to them?" Laurie asked.

"Why I imagine they've climbed out of the canyon and headed across the barrens," Noyes said. "But don't worry about them for a minute. Galway knows the barrens from one edge to another. You don't think—you don't think Galway kidnapped the girl?"

Her answer amused him. "If anything, it was the other way around."

"Is it a scandalous situation?"

"Neither was married, if that's what you mean. And before I turn bitter, I'd better tell you something."

His voice was gentle. "You couldn't be bitter."

"Thank you, Captain. But what I wanted to say was this. One of our people was a man named Mike Foss. Just before his death he admitted to me that he was the one who held up the Wickenburg stagecoach."

"The holdup for which Galway was tried?"

"Yes."

Noyes shook his head doubtfully. "If that could be proven, Galway could be cleared. But with only your word . . ."

"Would it help if he had told me where the missing money was hidden?"

He raised his head. "Without any question. If he told you that and if the money is there, I'd say Galway was free."

"Then the money is buried under Sam Rogell's house. Of course, Sam had nothing to do with it. That is . . ."

"We'll find out tomorrow," Noyes promised.

"But how will Jerd know?"

"He'll hear," Noyes said. "The news will sift through the Territory and some day he will hear that he doesn't have to hide any more. You're doing a fine thing for him. But what about you?"

"I—haven't any plans, yet."

His eyes brightened. Here was an attractive young woman. He was a widower and not an old man, still in his thirties. It would be nice to have a woman at the post again, someone to look after him, to make his life more endurable. If he could get a person like this girl here, he would be damned lucky. This was the time to work on her, too. He could sense that she was upset because Galway had disappeared with someone else. Because of that, her defenses might be down.

He stepped closer to her, touched her arm lightly and

said, "Laurie, if you haven't any plans, don't hurry them. Drift with the tide. I'll be around to help. I'm handy in lots of ways. Don't forget that for a minute."

She took a quick look at him, then looked away but didn't flinch from his touch on her arm.

"It's a nice evening," Noyes continued. "I'll walk you to your tent, but on the way I want to check with the sentries we've posted. If that would be all right."

He waited and was deeply pleased when she nodded. That wasn't much of a beginning but it was something.

The barrens, under the clear starlight, were a shadowy world. A steady wind blew in their faces as Midge and Jerd rode north on borrowed horses—borrowed from the Army. But then Jerd had taken them from those which had been captured from the Apaches and they might not be missed. Of course, if Captain Noyes decided to follow them, he could find their trail, but very probably Noyes was going to be busy with his prisoners. Jerd didn't think it very likely that anyone would come after them.

"You still could go back, Midge," he said gruffly.

She glanced at him. "Do you want me to?"

"Yes."

"Why, Jerd?"

"Because this is no kind of life for a woman."

"Tell me why it isn't."

"I don't have to," Jerd answered. "You're riding bareback, which isn't easy. We've no blankets, no water, no food. I have a food cache in the Mesquite hills, but that's two days away. It's a full day to water. It'll be a rough trip tomorrow, under the blazing sun."

"Suppose I make it? What then?"

"A day's rest, then I'll be heading for Prescott."

"We will," Midge corrected. "Why are we going to Prescott?"

"One of the passengers on the stagecoach which I supposedly held up lives in Prescott. He wasn't at my trial. He was off on a trip somewhere. He's my last chance."

"What if he can't help you?"

"Then it's Mexico, if I don't want to go to prison."

Midge smiled. "I always wanted to see Mexico."

"Now, that's a lie if I ever heard one," Jerd growled. "You have no interest in Mexico at all."

"You still want me to go back to Eden canyon."

"It's the only thing to do."

Midge stopped her horse. "All right. I think we ought to settle things, once and for all. Hobble the horses and get down for a minute."

Jerd slid to the ground. He hobbled the horses. Midge hadn't dismounted and now he turned to help her down, reaching up to lower her to the ground. She came down into his arms—and stayed there, her lips warm and ready for his kiss. Her body fitted against his. It was a ridiculous thing to believe she seemed to belong there, but that was the way it was. Her arms were tight around him, as strong as his.

Finally he pushed her away and scowled at her. "I thought we were going to talk."

"Do you still want me to go back?" Midge asked.

"Of course I don't. It's just . . ."

"Then we won't discuss the matter again. I'm going with you. Now, you'd better get the horses."

He laughed suddenly. Why fight a thing like this? If Midge had been able to stand the last three days, a rough trip across the barrens wasn't too much—and if they had to live in Mexico, why that's where they would go. He drew her into his arms again.

"This isn't—riding on," Midge said.

"No, but when we have to rest the horses, this is what will happen," Jerd said.

Midge was smiling. She made a perfect answer. "Rest them every hour."